to the Rescue

Look out for other books
by Julian Clary & David Roberts:

The Bolds

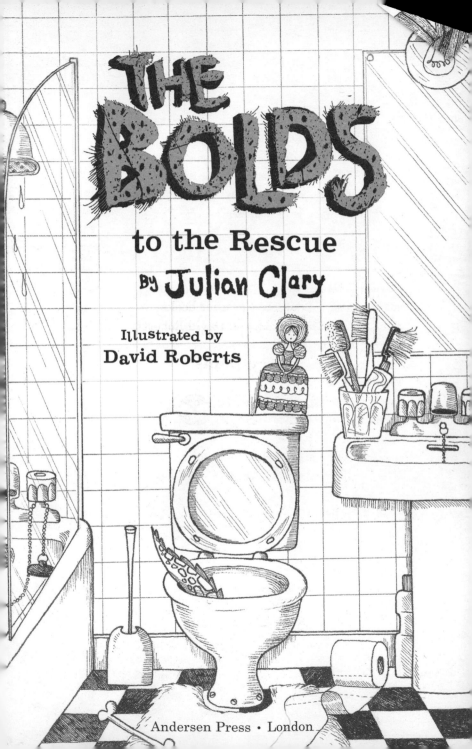

THE BOLDS

to the Rescue

BY Julian Clary

Illustrated by
David Roberts

Andersen Press · London

First published in 2016 by
Andersen Press Limited
20 Vauxhall Bridge Road
London SW1V 2SA
www.andersenpress.co.uk

2 4 6 8 10 9 7 5 3 1

British Library Cataloguing in Publication Data available.

Hardback ISBN 978 1 78344 449 6

Paperback ISBN 978 1 78344 380 2

Printed and bound in Great Britain by
Clays Limited, Bungay, Suffolk, NR35 1ED

For my parents,
Peter and Brenda Clary

JC

For my nephew,
Joel Roberts-Maloney

DR

Chapter

A word of warning before I start: it's probably best to keep this book away from grown-ups. They just won't understand it. They'll say it's 'a load of silly nonsense!' or ask, 'Why don't you read something more sensible?'

Well, grown-ups aren't always right. (I'm a grown-up myself, so I should know.) They read boring newspapers and tedious, thick books with no pictures and no jokes in them where nothing interesting happens, ever.

So much happens in THIS book, I'm not even sure where to begin. It is a very unusual book. As you are about to find out. But unusual doesn't mean it is silly or a load of nonsense. It is a true story. Make no mistake about it. You will understand that. Grown-ups won't.

And if a grown-up happens to be reading this to you as a bedtime story, then they must keep their remarks to themself.

There, then. I've got that off my chest, so let's begin.

Have you ever heard of the Bolds? I'm sure you probably have. They're a lovely family who live at 41 Fairfield Road in Teddington. They're always laughing, always joking. Mr Bold works in the local Christmas cracker factory, writing the jokes; Mrs Bold makes and sells elaborate hats at the local

market; and their twins, Betty and Bobby, are such sweet, adorable children.

Also living with them are Uncle Tony and Miranda, who they rescued from a safari park. Yes, that's right, a safari park – you did hear me correctly. Because the Bolds are a rather unusual family who do unusual things. We all have secrets, but their secret is BIGGER and hairier than most . . .

You see, behind closed doors they're not a family like yours or mine. A human family. Oh dear me, no. They're a family of hyenas pretending to be humans – from the tips of their furry ears right down to their paws.

No one knows. Except us.

You're probably in shock. Indeed, so was I when I first heard about them, but in actual fact it's not as shocking as you might think. There are a lot of animals out there living their lives pretending to be humans. Giraffes who stack shelves in Waitrose, pigs who eat popcorn noisily all the way through films in the cinema, bulldogs who work outside nightclubs. In fact, the Bolds' next-door neighbour, Mr McNumpty, is an animal too. A grizzly bear.

And whilst he and the Bolds have had their differences in the past, he's now firm friends with them and pops over most evenings for a game of dominoes and a couple of chops.

Except for Tuesdays. There are no games of dominoes that night because Tuesday nights in the Bolds' neat semi-detached house are very special. Tuesday nights are 'Grooming Night'. You might think this means face packs and manicures, but you'd be wrong: in fact the Bolds, and deaf old Uncle Tony, and Miranda the marmoset monkey, all sit in a circle, scratching, rubbing and nibbling each other, making sure all the loose fur comes out and any bits of mud or fluff that might be lurking there are removed. Not to mention the fleas . . .

Obviously they have to make sure the curtains are drawn and no one peeps in. Although we humans sometimes scratch and itch too, we aren't often seen lying on our backs while our mothers nibble at our tummies with sharp teeth, or found licking each other's ears with big, long tongues that reach right across our faces to the other ear and beyond.

Enjoyable and good for the Bolds as this is, the activity tickles too, so everyone at Number 41 ends up giggling and whooping with laughter. This just gets them in the mood to listen to some of Mr Bold's latest jokes:

Why did the banana go to the doctor?

Because he wasn't peeling well!

Or:

Why did the jelly wobble?

Because it saw
the milk shake!

And before long, on Tuesday nights in 41
Fairfield Road, everyone is rolling on the floor
in laughter.

Now, one Tuesday evening, once the grooming was done and the twins had gone to bed, Mrs Bold went to the bathroom to brush her teeth and wash and moisturise her friendly, furry face. The moment she sat on the toilet seat she thought she heard a faint cough followed by a splashing sound. She cocked her ear to one side and listened intently. Hyenas have very good hearing.

Then she blinked in confusion as she realised the sounds she was hearing were coming from beneath her . . . from inside the toilet bowl!

But before she could jump up to take a look she felt a little nip on her bottom.

'Shrieeek!' she cried, and shot up into the air. She then peered cautiously into the lavatory.

A head with two huge green eyes and a very long snout peered up at her, and in a deep, gravelly voice said: 'So sorry! It's only little me!'

Whatever this creature was, he or she seemed to have a LOT of teeth . . .

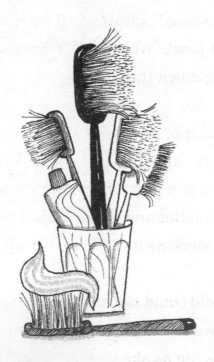

Chapter

'Good heavens!' said Mrs Bold, peering into the toilet bowl. 'Why? Who? What on earth are you doing down there?'

'Pardon me,' the voice said. 'I live down in the sewers, and I've had ENOUGH of it!' And with a bit of a groan the creature slid up and out of the toilet and then climbed out to sit on the seat, shaking its head to flick off the water.

Mrs Bold could see now that the unexpected visitor was a rather bewildered crocodile, almost as big as she was.

'That's better!' said the uninvited guest once she was dry. 'How do you do? I'm Sheila, and I'm a crocodile.'

'So I see!' said Mrs Bold, scratching her head. 'I'm Amelia Bold. Er, perhaps I'd better call my husband?'

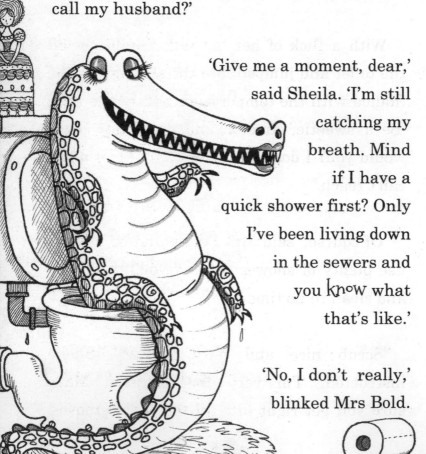

'Give me a moment, dear,' said Sheila. 'I'm still catching my breath. Mind if I have a quick shower first? Only I've been living down in the sewers and you know what that's like.'

'No, I don't really,' blinked Mrs Bold.

'Unspeakably filthy, that's what it's like. I'm sure I smell disgusting!'

'Well, now you mention it,' said Mrs Bold, her nose twitching at the pungent, shall we say 'earthy', aroma.

With a flick of her big tail, Sheila got off the toilet and jumped into the shower. As she fiddled with the temperature nozzle she said, 'Be a sweetie, Amelia, and scrub my back, would you? I don't have very long arms and I can't reach.'

'Of course,' said Mrs Bold obligingly. 'We'll use plenty of shower gel and you'll be lovely and clean in no time.'

'Scrub nice and hard, please,' Sheila instructed. 'I'm very thick-skinned. Make sure you get right into all the little grooves.

I've been swilling about in filth all my life. And while you're doing that, I'd better explain everything.'

'That would be nice,' said Mrs Bold as she set to work with a nailbrush on Sheila's knobbly back. Sheila was right – there was layer upon layer of dirt and muck, and considerable elbow grease was required.

'Ah! This is bliss!' sighed Sheila. And then she proceeded to tell her story to Mrs Bold. 'Before I begin, dear, am I right in thinking you are a hyena?'

'Well, if you put it like that, er, yes, I am,' said Mrs Bold, a bit shocked. 'But it's a secret.'

'Oh, I know.'

'You know? How do you know?'

'I'll come to that later,' said Sheila. 'Now, correct me if I'm wrong but a group of hyenas is known as a "clan", isn't it?'

'Yes!' agreed Mrs Bold. 'Though we are sometimes called a "cackle" of hyenas, which I think is a better description, certainly in our case. We really do love a good laugh.'

Sheila sniffed. 'Be that as it may. Do you know the name for a group of crocodiles, though?'

'No,' said Mrs Bold. 'I don't believe I do.'

'Well, dear, it's a "bask".'

'A bask of crocodiles?'

'Correct! And my point is that there are a LOT of crocodiles living in the sewers beneath

Teddington. BASKS of us. Been there for generations. How we got there no one really knows. It's suspected some rather eccentric human once had a pet crocodile who one day laid lots of eggs. When they all hatched out the human panicked. Flushed the babies down the lav to get rid of them and there we still are, blah, blah, blah.'

'How cruel!' gasped Mrs Bold.

'Yes, I agree. But humans can be, sometimes. There are a lot of goldfish down there too. Poor things don't stay gold for long, swimming through all that mess and manure . . .'

'Eew, yuck!' said Mrs Bold.

'Quite,' continued Sheila. 'Anyway, there we are. A bask of crocodiles living in dirt and darkness down in the sewers. We never see daylight, just the odd glimpse through a manhole cover maybe.'

'What do you poor things eat?'

'Rats, mainly. There are lots of rats down there. But life isn't much fun. Boring and smelly. Not much in the way of entertainment. We have to invent our own amusement. Which I did, when I was very young.'

'What did you do?'

'Well, we could all hear muffled conversations from the houses above, through the pipes. But then I discovered that I could swim up some pipes and round the S-bends and end up in people's bathrooms! As long as they weren't occupied at the time, I could have a bit of a break from sewer life.'

'You came up through people's toilets?'

'Yes, dear, I did! I was only young when I first did it, no bigger than your paw. I could have a few lungfuls of nice fresh air, listen in to some human conversations and then dive back down before anyone knew about it!'

'And no one ever discovered you?'

'Oh no. I have always been very careful about that. I've been popping in here for years. Long before *you* moved in . . .'

Mrs Bold stopped scrubbing for a moment while she took all this in. 'Oh,' she muttered

thoughtfully. 'So do you remember the people who lived here before us?'

'Well, yes I do, Amelia dear,' said Sheila, turning round to fix Amelia with a decidedly beady stare. 'Lovely couple. So in love. And looking forward to their holiday in Africa very much . . .'

'I see.'

'And then you and Mr Bold – Fred, isn't it? – came back from Africa instead of them. Very curious. A couple of hyenas, living in secret here in Teddington and pretending to be humans!'

Mrs Bold didn't know what to say.

'And then you had the twins, of course. Little Bobby and Betty. How are they?'

Mrs Bold was shocked. 'You know everything, then!' she gasped.

'Except what happened to the original HUMAN Fred and Amelia Bold? That's still a mystery to me. What did you do with them?'

'I can explain,' said the second Amelia Bold, feeling suddenly inexplicably guilty.

'Did you eat them, dear? Did you? Were they very tasty?' Sheila asked, her mouth visibly watering, saliva drooling down onto her chest.

'No, of course not! But we saw what happened to them, and it was very tragic and sad.'

'Ye-es?' Sheila tapped her foot impatiently on the side of the shower screen.

'They were out walking one day on holiday, got too hot and went for a swim in a watering hole. There were loud SNAPPING noises and then they were gone! Eaten, but not by us – by YOU!'

'Me?'

'Well, not actually you – you weren't there – but by some big hungry crocodiles.'

'Gosh!' exclaimed Sheila. 'What an uncanny coincidence. Some crocodiles have got no sense of restraint.'

'So then my husband and I put on their clothes and pretended we were – or are – Fred and Amelia Bold. I fancied a change of life and it seemed like a great opportunity.'

'I see, of course. Well, what a remarkable stroke of luck for you both. Waste not, want not. Carry on with the scrubbing, dear. I'm feeling much better already.'

'So have you been listening to us from the toilet for some time?' asked Mrs Bold, resuming her work and wondering where this was all leading.

'I have, yes. By far my favourite house, this is. Some people live such dreary lives. Barely speak to each other! But not you lot. Never a dull moment at 41 Fairfield Road. Pass me a towel, dear, I think that's enough scrubbing for now. A nice white fluffy one, please.'

Just then there was a tap on the bathroom door.

Sheila wrapped herself in a bath towel and wound another, smaller towel around her head like a turban. 'Not one of his best,' she muttered. 'You'd better introduce me.'

Mrs Bold unlocked the bathroom door and Mr Bold came in smiling cheerfully.

Where do bees go to the bathroom?

At the BP station! And—

'Fred,' interrupted Mrs Bold. 'Meet Sheila. She's a crocodile who, er, just popped up through the toilet for a quick visit.'

Fred looked a little surprised, then shrugged as he looked at Sheila swathed in towels. He shook her claw, and said, 'Pleased to meet you, Sheila.'

'She needed a shower,' explained Mrs Bold. 'It's not very nice down in the sewers . . .'

What do you call a sewer expert?

A conna-sewer!

Mr Bold paused while Sheila laughed politely.

'How do you do, Mr Bold. Charmed, I'm sure,' she said, her smile revealing her many rows of huge sharp teeth.

'Well, I'm very pleased to meet you too, Sheila. Glad you've enjoyed a nice shower. Do drop in anytime.'

'Sheila has been dropping in for years, apparently,' explained Mrs Bold, a slight quiver creeping into her voice. 'She knows . . . everything . . . about us. And where we come from.'

'Ahem. I see,' said Mr Bold, suddenly as nervous as his wife that their secret was out.

'And what is more,' growled Sheila, 'I'm not "popping in" this time. I'm staying put. I know all about poor Tony and tasty – I mean tiny – Miranda the monkey. The kindness you showed in rescuing them from the safari park is legendary down in the sewers. You help animals in need. You teach them to blend in as humans. You are saints, you really are!'

'Staying put?' said Mrs Bold, confused.

'Yes, dear. I'm moving in. Aren't you THRILLED?'

'Well, I—'

'The thing is, dear Amelia,' Sheila interrupted, 'I'm a growing croc. I only just managed to squeeze round the S-bend this time. Another few days, a few more rats, another couple of centimetres wider and I'd get stuck. You wouldn't want that now, would you?' A couple of crocodile tears slid down her face.

'Well, I-I-I . . .' stammered Amelia.

'I'm moving in with you Bolds. Temporarily. You can teach me how to "pass" as a human – just like *you* do – and then I'll be on my way. I could get a job as a lifeguard, perhaps?' Sheila cackled at the thought. 'What a marvellous service you Bolds provide. You're the talk of the animal kingdom, my dears!'

'But I'm not sure we can—' began Mr Bold.

'Nonsense!' cried Sheila. 'This crocodile is here to STAY! That is settled. Now, get me a snack, would you, Fred? Got any tuna fish? Or sausages, perhaps? I'm starving!'

'Er, I'll see what I can find,' said Fred, backing out of the bathroom.

'Amelia, dear? Isn't it time for some full body moisturiser?' cooed Sheila, as she raised her arms in readiness. 'My poor skin is desperate after all those years in the sewer. Drier than a camel's, er, tongue. Be gentle with me, dear!'

And so it was that the Bold household acquired a new lodger. And a rather snappy one at that. Sheila took up residence in the bathroom, helping herself to baths every few hours and getting through an awful lot of hot water, shower gel and clean towels.

But the Bolds were too kind to ask her to leave.

And Sheila was right – the Bolds were indeed the talk of the animal kingdom. Word had got out somehow that 41 Fairfield Road was a safe haven for any animal who wanted to make the 'jump' and start a new life as a human. Very soon other animals started arriving, all wanting to learn how to walk and talk and get jobs like people do.

And as you will discover, the house was about to get very crowded indeed . . .

Chapter

A few days after Sheila's arrival, Nigel McNumpty, the Bolds' next-door neighbour, was strolling along Fairfield Road with his friend, Uncle Tony. They had enjoyed an ice cream each in Bushy Park, and were walking home in contented silence.

Nigel, who had a keen sense of smell, being a grizzly bear, suddenly became aware that someone was following them. He stopped and looked behind him, and saw an elegant apricot-coloured poodle gazing longingly at him.

'What have we here? Are you lost, little dog?' he asked.

Tony turned next and, although already stooped due to his age and arthritis, he stooped a bit more to pet the dog. 'Nice dog,' he said. 'Where do you live, then?'

'*Je suis destitute!*' said the poodle in a strong French accent. 'I am homeless!'

'Oh dear!' said Mr McNumpty. 'You poor little dog. What is your name?'

'I am Fifi Lampadaire,' replied the dog, tears welling up in her eyes. 'Please – 'elp me!'

'But of course we will!' said Tony. 'Don't worry, little lost dog. Come home with us and we'll call the dogs home.'

Fifi trotted along with the two old boys, glad that her plan was working. So far so good.

Once they got back to Mr McNumpty's house, the two friends gave Fifi a bowl of water and found her some biscuits in the larder, which she ate, but with little enthusiasm.

'Thank you. Merci,' said Fifi. 'A little stale, but acceptable.'

'You speak French and English? Quite unusual!' said Mr McNumpty. 'You must be a very talented dog!'

'Mais oui! Of course,' agreed Fifi, settling herself on a sofa. 'And now I 'ave to tell you the truth. I am not homeless. I am seeking refuge here. I throw myself on your mercy, *messieurs*! I will not leave.' And indeed Fifi rolled on her back to prove her point.

Tony and Mr McNumpty looked from the dog to each other in astonishment.

'What do you mean, Fifi?'

'I want to live with the Bolds. I think they can 'elp me. You see, I 'ave heard about them. Animals helping animals to better themselves. Teaching them 'ow to live like humans. This is what I want. I am Fifi Lampadaire, a star of the future!'

'Well, it's true the Bolds are very kind people,' began Tony. 'But I don't know—'

'Please ask them to let me stay!' pleaded Fifi. 'Please, I beg of you. It will not be for the eternity, just until my talent is discovered and my star can rise brightly in the sky!'

'What is your talent then?' asked Mr McNumpty bluntly.

'I am a singer, a singer *extraordinaire!*' exclaimed Fifi, gazing up to the heavens. 'It is what I live for. The love songs, the ballads, you know?'

'Goodness. Most unusual in a dog!' exclaimed Tony.

'Oui. It is true. No one will take a singing dog seriously. My last owners, they just threw the bucket of water over me whenever I began a song.'

'How very unkind!' said Mr McNumpty.

'This is why I need the Bolds to 'elp me. I am a singer trapped in a dog's body. They could teach me to walk and act like a human being and I will launch my career and leave them in peace while I go on a world tour.'

'Sounds reasonable enough,' said Tony. 'There are animal rights, just as there are human rights. You have a right to sing, young Fifi, a right to express yourself!'

Fifi wagged her tail enthusiastically and gave Tony an affectionate lick on his face. 'Merci, Monsieur Tony, thank you. Merci beaucoup!'

'You'll have to learn not to wag and lick, though,' observed Mr McNumpty. 'And before we do anything else we had better speak to Mr and Mrs Bold. Their house is quite full, you know, especially since Sheila the crocodile arrived. They might think there isn't enough room.'

Fifi looked crestfallen for a moment, but then she had an idea. 'Ouvrez la fenêtre, s'il vous plaît,' she said.

'Come again?' asked Mr McNumpty.

'Pardon!' said Fifi. 'Could you open the window, please? I will unleash my talent and for sure they will not be able to refuse me!'

'Good plan,' agreed Tony. 'Clever dog. And you can always stay in *my* room with *me*. Provided Fred and Amelia agree, of course.'

Next door, Mr and Mrs Bold were sitting on their garden swing, talking about Sheila.

'Her mouth is so huge, I'm going to have to buy a new toilet brush to clean her teeth with,' Mrs Bold was saying.

What does a crocodile call children?

Appetisers!

'Stop it!' said Mrs Bold. 'You know I'm a little nervous about having her around Betty and Bobby.'

The twins were playing beside them on the lawn. 'Don't worry, Mum, Sheila's all right,' said Bobby.

'Yes, I like having her around,' said Betty. 'And she wants us to take her down to Teddington Lock one evening when no one is about, so she can go for a swim in the River Thames. Would that be OK?'

'What do you think, Fred?' asked Mrs Bold.

'Well, that would be rather daring. It must be a bit cramped in the bath for her, but I'm not sure it's safe having her swimming out in public.'

At that moment their conversation was interrupted by a beautiful, trembling voice wafting over the fence, singing:

'*Paris in the sunshine*
Oh, nothing can compare!
You can go for your holidays
And eat fresh croissants there.'

'Goodness, how lovely is that?' sighed Mrs Bold. 'Sending shivers down my spine.'

Why did the singer climb the ladder?

To reach the high notes!

'Hush, Dad,' said Betty. 'It's coming from Mr McNumpty's house. Do you think he's got the radio on?'

'I don't think so,' said Bobby, listening intently now. 'There's no music, just that fabulous voice.' They all listened, transfixed for a few moments, as the song continued.

'Paris in the moonlight
Please make no mistake,
It is a city of romance
And very nice sirloin steak.'

Eventually Mr Bold
jumped up to look over the fence.
'Good lord!' he said to his family. 'Nigel's got a singing poodle in there!'

And that is how Fifi came to be introduced to the Bolds. Of course they fell in love with her charming voice, and agreed to help her in any way they could. A talent like that should not be hidden away and they're a very special family, as I've told you before.

So now there was Mr and Mrs Bold, the twins, Uncle Tony, Miranda the marmoset monkey, Sheila the crocodile and Fifi the French poodle, all living at Number 41 Fairfield Road.

You might think there wasn't room for any more waifs and strays. But guess what? You'd be wrong . . .

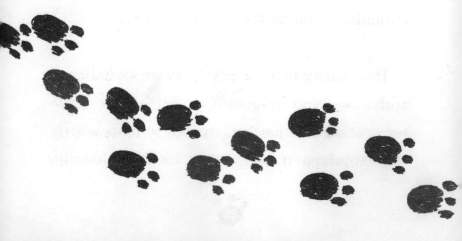

Chapter

So how come all these animals had suddenly started arriving at the Bolds' house? Well, you need to remember that human beings – like you and I – think we are the cleverest creatures on the planet. We think we know all the answers, but quite frankly we don't. And one thing we don't know much about is how animals communicate with each other.

They speak to each other, of course, barking and squeaking or growling, and as we have seen, they are perfectly capable of learning our language if they need to. But they do other strange things too: bees dance in different directions to tell their friends where the best food is. Chameleons change colour; whales sing!

So when word got round about the Bolds' life in Teddington and the daring rescue of poor Tony from the safari park, it was headline news in the animal world. Furthermore, any animal unhappy with his or her lot in life began to dream of paying the Bolds a visit, to see if perhaps these kind hyenas could help them to start a new, exciting life. And of course, after Sheila and Fifi arrived at Number 41 and were allowed to stay, moving in with the Bolds became all the rage. A pregnant cat slipped in through the back door one day and had six adorable kittens in the airing cupboard.

She made it clear she didn't want to learn how to live like a **human** though. She just wanted somewhere safe and warm to live.

A week later a **turtle** made himself at home in the washing machine, and a flock of at least fifteen **seagulls** flew in from the Isle of Wight and perched on the Bolds' windowsills, peering in at them, squawking and banging on the windows with their wings. (Fortunately they didn't want to move into the house – they were just nosy. **Nosy** and **noisy** and **messy**, but the Bolds didn't mind.)

One morning a sheep called Roger, who had a black face and magnificent curly horns, appeared in the front garden.

'I can't face another winter in a field, buried in the snow. Honestly, I can't,' he explained to the twins, who'd opened the door to him. 'Do you think I might be allowed to stay here?'

'Well, I'll have to ask my mum,' said Betty. 'But I don't see why not. We can't say yes to some animals and no to others.'

Roger's eyes filled with tears of gratitude. 'I'd like to give living as a human a try, if I might. Do you think your family could teach me?'

'Can you walk on your back legs?' said Bobby.

'Oh yes, I can do that easily,' said Roger, and he raised himself up in a trice.

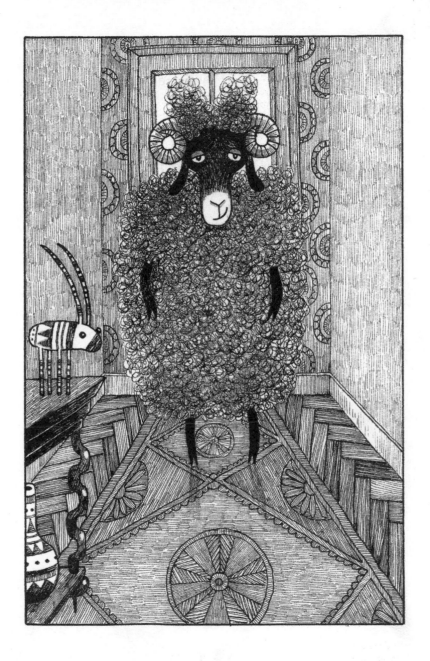

'And what sort of human job do you fancy?' was Bobby's next question.

'Well, I've given it some thought,' said Roger. 'And the truth is, although I'm a sheep, for some reason I'm not very outdoorsy.'

'No wonder you wanted a change!' said Betty sympathetically.

'I'm rather fond of children though. Played for hours with the lambs in springtime. Maybe I could earn my sheep – sorry, keep – by babysitting for your parents to start with? Eventually I'd like to work as a nanny or au pair, perhaps.'

'You've thought all this through!' said Bobby admiringly.

'Oh yes. Thought about it for years.'

'A sheep! What fun!' said Mr Bold when he met Roger.

'He'd like to stay,' explained Betty. 'He says he'll babysit us if you want to have a night out sometime.'

'That would be rather nice, Fred,' said Mrs Bold. 'I feel like we never have any time to ourselves now the house is so full.'

'And he can walk on his back legs already,' Bobby pointed out. 'So you wouldn't have to teach him much.'

'Yes, of course he can stay!' said Mr Bold. 'Welcome to the madhouse, Roger! Glad to have you aboard. Space is getting tight but I believe there might be a free corner in the dining room.'

He paused, then added with a grin:

What do you get if you cross an angry sheep with a grumpy cow?

An animal that's in a baaaaaad moooood!

'You'll get used to Dad's jokes,' said Betty, giving Roger's woolly back a reassuring rub.

Realising that the Bolds' house was now very full, Mr McNumpty kindly offered to accommodate Roger in his back bedroom. And before too long it was also decided to take down the fence between the back gardens of Numbers 41 and 39 to give some of the larger animals more room to move about. There was a lot of coming and going between the two houses and this made it easier.

Before long both houses were overcrowded and more than a little untidy, but everyone got along fine, although Sheila could be a little bad-tempered if the hot water ran out. Mealtimes were not very well-mannered occasions however – but perhaps it's the same in your home too. Certainly knives and forks had not been mastered yet, nor had 'please' and 'thank you' and food quite often ended up sliding down the walls.

'If these animals want to blend in then we will have to teach them how to eat more politely,' said Mrs Bold half-heartedly.

'Just put a little bit in your mouth at a time, Fifi. No need to gulp things down in one go!'

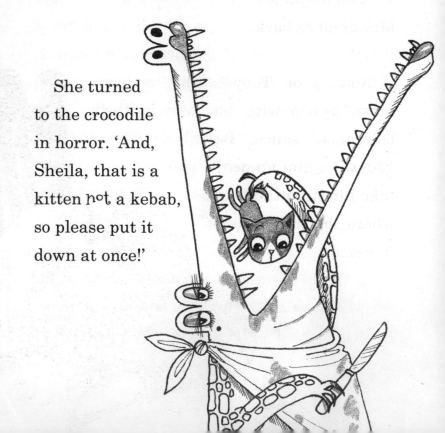

She turned to the crocodile in horror. 'And, Sheila, that is a kitten not a kebab, so please put it down at once!'

Then she
saw Bobby.
'Stop winding
spaghetti round
Roger's horns
please, Bobby! And
you should know
better than to wipe
your hands on Mr
McNumpty's back.

'Now, poor Tony seems to have
fallen asleep with his nose in the
bolognaise sauce. Betty, could
you wake him up gently and
take him into the lounge
where he can snooze
in peace?

'And could the seagulls please stop doing their business all over the curtains?' she went on. 'If the Isle of Wight posse are peckish, there's no need to scavenge: there's some pepperoni and mozzarella cheese hanging from the light fitting. Help yourselves to that!'

'Don't fret so much, dear,' said Mr Bold to his wife. 'This is the one place where we can all behave like animals. I'm rather loving the noise and the mess myself!'

'Oh, I am too, I am!' laughed Mrs Bold.

'And no one is taking any notice of me anyway, let's face it! But unless we want these animals living with us for the rest of our lives, we really do need to teach them how to eat and behave like humans or they'll never be able to move on.'

'Would it be OK if Minnie came for tea soon and met everyone?' asked Betty. Minnie was Betty's best friend from school and she knew all about the Bolds' secret identity. In fact, she was the only human who knew the truth about the Bold family, but she was a good friend and had never told anyone.

'Oh, I don't know,' said Mrs Bold. 'I love Minnie dearly and it would be lovely to see her, but I feel a little anxious about her coming round when there's a crocodile in the house. Don't forget what happened to the previous Mr and Mrs Bold.'

Suddenly there was a loud KNOCK at the front door.

'Hmmm,' said Mr Bold. 'If you ask me, that noise was made from a h∞f, not a hand or a paw. Let's see if I'm right.'

Chapter

Mr Bold went into the hall and Betty and Bobby followed him curiously. As he opened the door they were shocked to see two rather odd creatures, their faces barely visible beneath blankets wrapped around their heads like nuns' wimples.

'Good evening. Can I help you, er, ladies?' asked Mr Bold brightly.

'Mr Bold?' whispered the one on the left, revealing a glimpse of two large, frightened eyes.

'Yes, correct!'

'Oh, thank goodness. Please let us in before
he catches us.' Both visitors glanced nervously
up Fairfield Road and looked pleadingly at
Mr Bold and the twins.

'Come in at once,' said Mr Bold, opening the door wide.

There was a whinny of relief from beneath the blankets and a cloud of dusty breath.

'Thank you, thank you so much,' said the one who hadn't spoken yet, and Mr Bold ushered them into the lounge, which was empty apart from Uncle Tony asleep in an armchair – a red, meaty residue drying into a thick crust around his wispy beard, and Miranda the marmoset monkey curled up on his lap. Her eyes opened WIDE in astonishment as she saw who was entering the room.

Something in the fearful look of the strangers made Bobby and Betty glance out the window, although they had no idea what they were so scared of.

'No one there. You're safe now,' Betty said reassuringly.

'Who are you and how can I help?' her father asked the new arrivals.

The guests looked relieved, then shook the blankets off their heads to reveal fine equine features, beautiful, deep shining eyes and magnificent, flowing manes.

'Horses!' cried Bobby.

'I say!' exclaimed Mr Bold and then, inevitably:

What do you give a sick horse?

Horse stirrup!

'I'm sure that's a very funny joke, but I'm afraid we're too upset to laugh at the moment,' said the larger of the two horses. 'We're a bit jittery.'

'I'm sorry. Couldn't help myself,' smiled Mr Bold as he admired the two fine horses now standing in his lounge, their rippling muscles quivering with nerves.

The bigger one was a shiny black all over, with just a dash of white on his forehead, and his female friend was a light honey-colour with a golden mane and long legs.

'I'm Gangster's Moll,' she said, bowing her head. 'And this is Minty Boy.'

'Delighted,' said Minty Boy, still glancing around him as if someone or something might leap out and grab him at any moment.

'Please try and relax,' said Mr Bold. 'What is it you're both so frightened of?'

Minty Boy rolled his eyes with the horror of it all. 'Oh dear, Mr Bold, you have no idea what we've been though!'

'Awful! Terrible! Unspeakable!' agreed Gangster's Moll, her voice louder and higher with each word.

'Please calm down, the pair of you,' said Mr Bold. 'You can tell me all about it later. Meanwhile, would you like something to eat or drink? Might help to settle you. Betty, go and ask your mother whether there's any of that carrot risotto left. Bobby, see if you can find a bucket of water.' Mr Bold could see that the new arrivals were of a nervous, highly-strung disposition.

'Have you got a garden?' asked Minty Boy, his back legs crossing one over the other.

'Yes. Just out the back,' said Mr Bold. 'Let me show you the way.'

'Thank you. I haven't been since we left Cheltenham. What I need to do will be very good for your roses . . .'

'Ah, Cheltenham, where the racecourse is?'

asked Mr Bold. 'Just as I figured. You two are racehorses, aren't you?'

'Indeed we are, Mr Bold. And we desperately need your help.'

Chapter

Once the handsome stallion and the beautiful mare had made themselves comfortable in the garden, they returned to the lounge – where all the other members of the household (and Number 39) filed in to meet them. Mr and Mrs Bold, Bobby and Betty, Mr McNumpty, Uncle Tony and Miranda, Sheila the crocodile, Fifi the French poodle, Roger the sheep, not to mention the cat and her kittens, the turtle and the seagulls, all sat cross-legged on the floor in front of them, eager to hear their story.

'So,' said Mr Bold, clearing his throat as if introducing the next act at a cabaret evening.

'Very nice to see everyone. Er . . . we're very pleased to welcome Minty Boy and Gangster's Moll into our neighhh-bourhood! Let's hear it, please!' There was even a slight smattering of applause, which sounded rather different from human applause due to the fact that fur, claws and hooves slapped together don't sound the same as hands.

'Hello, everyone,' began Gangster's Moll nervously, hiding her eyes under her heavy mane. 'We are just so relieved to be here. We heard about the Bolds' safe house through the animal grapevine, of course.' She looked gratefully towards Mr and Mrs Bold. 'Without you, I don't know what we would have done or where we would have gone—'

'We'd be horsemeat!' interrupted Minty Boy, his dark eyes flashing with anger at the thought.

There was a gasp of shock from Miranda and Roger, but a rather distasteful slurp of anticipation from Sheila. Mrs Bold shot the croc a warning glare.

Gangster's Moll took a deep breath and continued. 'We grew up together. Practically brother and sister. Never been parted. As you may have guessed we are both thoroughbred racehorses, born from a long line of champions on both sides. My mother was ridden by Lester Piggott.'

'Some folk have all the luck,' muttered Minty Boy.

'Anyway. We were "owned" by a posh, heartless, nasty man who paid thousands of pounds for us.'

'More fool him,' snorted Minty Boy, who

then took over the story. 'Unfortunately we just don't like racing. We don't know why. Not cut out for it. Just one of those things.'

'It is such hard work!' sighed Moll.

'Our owner – Tarquin Twit-Twot – was furious with us,' continued Minty Boy. 'He thought if he was unkind to us and taught his jockeys to use whips on us, we'd win races and earn him lots of money. But no. We didn't.'

'Everything came to a head at Cheltenham racecourse this afternoon,' said Gangster's Moll. 'It was the Gold Cup race. We were both entered and Tarquin made it very clear that we were to win first and second place – or else.' She paused to take a few deep breaths. 'We came joint last. We strolled over the finishing line about ten minutes after all the other horses, chewing grass without a care in the world.

The crowd in the stand roared with laughter.'

'Hurrah for you!' piped up Miranda.

'Well, yes,' said Gangster's Moll, biting her lip. 'But Tarquin didn't see it that way.'

'He was totally humiliated. Red in the face, in fact,' said Minty Boy, shuddering at the memory. 'He stormed into our stable and was about to take his whip to us, but there were other people around so he couldn't.'

'So he did something far worse,' continued Gangster's Moll. 'He sold us. Sold us in the Cheltenham car park, to a grubby little man, for just a couple of hundred pounds!'

'Quel dommage!' sighed Fifi. 'What a shame.'

'It gets worse,' said Minty Boy. 'This man – his name is Dodgy Dean – had only one plan for us. To serve us up with chips and peas in a restaurant in Belgium!'

There was a yelp of alarm from everyone in the room. Except Sheila, surprisingly enough.

'I know!' said Gangster's Moll. 'Can you imagine? Belgium! We were being driven down the motorway on our way to the ferry when Dodgy Dean had to stop for petrol. We knew it was our only chance. We used all our strength to kick down the door of the horsebox and we ran all the way here. Faster than we've ever wanted to run before. But Dean followed us. We tried to hide, but that isn't easy when you are a racehorse.'

'So Dodgy Dean is hunting for you now?' concluded Mr McNumpty.

Minty Boy looked faint at the mention of the name. 'He will be searching everywhere,' he said, shaking his head. 'He paid money for us and won't be happy until he's sold us on to be made into horsey lasagne.'

'We managed to give him the slip on Teddington High Street, but he knows we are around here somewhere!' added Gangster's Moll. 'We'd be very tasty served up on plates, apparently,' she said bitterly. 'And there are hungry Belgians wanting their dinner.'

'I'm going out to look for him,' announced Uncle Tony bravely, wincing as he got to his feet. 'I'll show him my teeth and he won't come back here in a hurry.'

'Maybe that isn't such a good idea,' said Mrs Bold soothingly. 'Your teeth aren't as scary as they once were . . .'

'Neither of them!' said Bobby.

'Cheeky blighter,' muttered poor Tony as he sat back down again.

Mr Bold seized the opportunity to cheer everyone up with a joke:

What happened to the man who put his false teeth in backwards?

He ate himself!

'Now listen up,' said Mr McNumpty, once the laughter had died down. 'This is serious. Outside of this house, no one must say a word about our new friends. We must all act normally – or as normally as we can. With any luck Dodgy Dean will give up and go home eventually.'

'I doubt that very much,' said Gangster's Moll with a sigh that turned into a big horsey yawn. 'But maybe there is a chance that you're right.'

'Now – on a more practical note,' said Mrs Bold, realising how tired the latest housemates were, 'where are you going to sleep?'

'Well, being horses, we don't need to lie down to sleep,' explained Minty Boy. 'We can sleep standing up – so anywhere will do.'

'Then you can stay here in the lounge,' Mr Bold decided.

'Perfect!' said Gangster's Moll, her eyes beginning to close already.

How do you make a baby sleep on a space ship?

You rocket!

Realising that their new friends were too tired to cope with any more of Mr Bold's jokes, everyone crept out of the lounge and left them to sleep.

Apart from Miranda, who decided to curl up on the windowsill and keep a lookout, just in case the burly horse trader – or anyone else – came sniffing about.

Chapter

Word must have got round the animal kingdom that 41 Fairfield Road (not to mention 39) was full to the brim, for the time being at least, as no more animals seeking refuge arrived over the next few days.

Everyone got to know each other, and although it was more than a little crowded in the two houses, Mr Bold made sure everyone kept laughing all day.

But fun though it all was, life in the two houses in Fairfield Road was terribly messy and noisy.

'I think, dear,' said Mrs Bold to her husband as they got into bed after another hectic day, 'we need to be a bit more organised.'

'Oh dear,' said Fred. 'That sounds very human.'

'Well, yes it does. But after all, we are supposed to be helping all these animals to live like humans eventually, and quite frankly, this place is like a rather badly run ZOO. We have responsibilities, you know. We need to get cracking.'

Did you hear the joke about the broken egg?

Yes, it cracked me up!

'Let's try and be serious for a moment, dear. We can't carry on like this. We can't afford to feed everyone for a start. Our food bill is ridiculously big now. That Minty eats like a . . . well, he eats like a horse. And everyone needs clothes and shoes if we're going to teach them how to be humans. We're forgetting what they all came here for. We need to give them lessons – formal lessons – in how to be human, and then they need to move on!'

'Ugh! Lessons?' answered her husband, pulling a face.

Why did the teacher turn the lights on?

Because her pupils were so DIM!

Mrs Bold then took out a pen and paper, and together – between jokes – she and her husband wrote out a timetable of classes and daily events that would help all the different animals achieve their ambition of living in the human world.

'That's more like it!' said Mrs Bold as she stuck a notice on the fridge door for everyone to see the next morning:

IMPORTANT MEETING
TOMORROW
at 10 a.m.!!
EVERYONE MUST
ATTEND!

'This is going to be So much better for us all.'

'And fun?' asked Mr Bold doubtfully.

'Of course!' she replied, giving his ear an affectionate stroke. 'Everything is always fun when you're around, dear.'

Mr Bold blushed underneath his furry face.

The next morning at 10 a.m., Mr Bold called everyone into the kitchen, cleared his throat and addressed his audience: 'As you know, Amelia and I love having you all here and are flattered that you feel safe in our house and want to live like us. But the truth is that money and space are getting tight and we're struggling to feed everyone on our wages. I think we're all agreed that the sooner you can get on and start living your lives as humans and earning your own money, the better.'

'Well, I'm sorry if we're a burden to you,' said Sheila rather grumpily.

'Now you know that's not what I'm saying,' said Mr Bold. 'But we need to face facts. Amelia and I can't afford to feed and clothe you all forever and there is going to come a point when some of you need to move on. That's why you came here, after all – we're just a stop along the way, not your final destination. How long before someone discovers I have two racehorses living in my lounge and doing their business in my garden?'

'We do have lovely roses now though, thanks to them,' Roger pointed out.

'Indeed, indeed. But you all need to learn how to live like humans and then you need to, er, go and do it somewhere bigger.'

'You're right, Mr Bold,' said Roger. 'I want to work with children, I don't want to sit around here all day making a mess and hiding away.'

'And I want to be a star,' said Fifi. 'I won't be young and beautiful for ever. I need to make the most of my talents now.'

'Well, we've devised a timetable,' said Mrs Bold. 'From now on we're going to have formal lessons every day.'

'What about me and Bobby?' asked Betty.

'No, dear. You two will be in school, but your father and I are going to arrange our jobs so that we can run this place like a school too.'

'Great,' said Bobby miserably. 'I'm going to live *in* a school and then spend all day *at* school.'

Mrs Bold gave Bobby a sympathetic glance, then looked over at the assorted animals. 'Now for those of you who can't read yet, Mr Bold is going to read out the new timetable,' she said. 'But copies will be posted up around the house.'

And so the timetable was read out:

8 a.m. Table Manners

* How to master knives, forks and spoons.
* Napkins – these are for wiping your mouth, please note, and not to put on your head or wipe your bottoms with!

9 a.m. Walking on Hind Legs

* All about balance. Tricky to begin with, but essential if you are to appear in public.
* (Humans are rarely seen on all fours, unless very young, drunk, or doing yoga classes.)

10 a.m. Toilet Training

* Unlike us animals, humans don't just go to the toilet anywhere they feel the need. In this lesson we will teach you bladder and bowel control, how to use the toilet facility, sit on the toilet seat, use toilet paper and 'flush' when you've finished.
* Humans are also very keen on washing their hands afterwards, please note.
* (A bucket and shovel will be available for those who haven't quite got the hang of things yet.)

11 a.m. Break

* Much-needed downtime! Feel free to revert to your natural animal ways and follow your instincts. (Although, Sheila, this doesn't mean eating any of the smaller house guests!)

* Snacks of bones, fruit and hay will be available.

11.30 a.m. Speech Therapy and Reading

* Almost as important as walking convincingly like a human is talking like one. Our animal snouts, extra teeth or long tongues make this difficult sometimes, but not impossible. Persevere!

* Try some of these fun tongue twisters:

'Eleven owls licked eleven little liquorice lollipops!'

'The big bug bit the little beetle, but the little beetle bit the big bug back.'

12.30 p.m. Lunch

🐾 Lunch will be taken 'human style' using all the things we have learned in the morning.

🐾 We will sit round the table, using cutlery like people do, chatting politely about the weather, and then use the lavatory if necessary.

1.30 p.m. Playtime

🐾 You may be an animal again for the next hour. Enjoy yourself!

🐾 (N.B. No biting or scratching, please. Loud animal noises should be made in the airing cupboard to avoid disturbing the neighbourhood.)

2.30 p.m. Careers Advice

🐾 Sooner or later you're going to have to get a job. Each housemate's abilities and preferences will be assessed to see what career might best suit them.

🐾 We will also practise interview techniques.

🐾 If we think you're ready for it, a trip to the Teddington Job Centre will be arranged to check out local vacancies in your field.

3.30 p.m. Dressing Up

* This is one of the more peculiar aspects
of human behaviour: they like to wear
trousers, shirts, dresses, skirts, shoes,
hats, coats etc, almost all the time. Not to
mention underwear. It's all very odd, but if
we are to blend in, then it is essential we
look the part.
(Also, clothes are handy for hiding naughty
tails, ears, hairy backs, scaly skin and
so on.)

* We have bought a large collection of clothes
from local charity shops, and we are bound
to have something to fit you, whatever
your size or shape. We will teach you how
to 'zip', 'button' and 'belt up' and help you
decide which colours and styles best suit
you . . . No good wearing a mini skirt if
you're a big muscly stallion, for example!

4.30 p.m. Emergency Drill - TOP SECRET!

- ❧ We have to be mindful of the fact that we are animals living in secret here. Although we are doing nothing wrong, humans are a funny lot, and if they find out they might interfere – or worse still, make us all go back to our previous way of life. Or even worse, send us away to live in a zoo.

- ❧ Behind these closed doors we are safe, but what if some humans come in one day? The gas man to read the meter, for example? Or a Jehovah's Witness might knock on the door . . . We must be prepared.

- ❧ In this class we will prepare for human interference or invasion and make a plan so that nothing and no one looks out of place to prying eyes . . .

5.30 p.m. Group Therapy

- ❧ Some animals take to the human style of living very easily, but for others, leaving their old life behind proves difficult sometimes, even upsetting.

🐾 This daily session gives us all a chance to share our worries, hopes and fears. We **can** support each other. After all we are all in this together, remember. Have strength, brothers and sisters!

After the notice was read out, everyone cheered and clapped. This was going to be fun, and a brighter, exciting future for everyone was beginning to take shape!

Chapter

With the new timetable in place, soon the Bolds' house was a busy, but happy one. Just like lessons in school, not everyone could be good at everything of course – apart from Fifi, who was top of the class in all subjects. She had fabulous conversation skills even before she arrived at Fairfield Road and had been walking on her hind legs since she was a puppy. She not only used the toilet daintily but insisted on locking the door while she did so. ('This is a moment privé!')

She could speak fluently in several languages (including Dog, obviously) and liked nothing more than to curl up and read a good book in the evenings. (She was halfway through *101 Dalmatians* by Dodie Smith.)

'But of course. I am a French poodle – the most intelligent breed of dog!' she shrugged in her thick, French accent.

And as you can imagine, Fifi loved the Dressing Up lesson, picking out anything sparkly or made of silk before anyone else could get their paws on it.

'I cannot wear the man-made fibres, malheureusement. They give me the itch!' she said.

As for the Group Therapy sessions – after Fifi stood up and expressed her feelings by singing a medley of three very sad French songs, Mrs Bold had no choice but to interfere.

'Thank you, Fifi dear. I think we catch the drift. Lovely as your singing is, perhaps we could open the discussion up to everyone *else* now?' Fifi sat down in a huff. There wasn't an awful lot more the Bolds could teach her – they just needed to help her have her talent 'discovered'.

Sheila the crocodile managed very well in the Walking-on-Hind-Legs lesson, but only with the help of her big, strong tail, which inevitably stretched out on the ground behind her. If she tried to hide her tail she keeled over immediately and once broke a tooth in the process. Mrs Bold solved this balance problem by finding a long, velvet maxi skirt in the dressing-up box, which covered Sheila's tail completely.

'You'll just have to present yourself as a bit of a hippy, dear. Try this big floppy hat to go with it . . . Excellent! Distracts from your rather, er, generous jawline too.'

Table Manners was a harder lesson for Sheila: 'I keep eating the cutlery – just can't help myself. That's the third fork I've chomped my way through this morning! If only I could nibble rather than snap!'

Mr Bold interrupted:

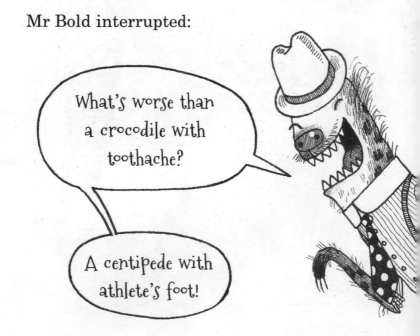

What's worse than a crocodile with toothache?

A centipede with athlete's foot!

Roger the sheep, it has to be said, was a little dozy and had trouble concentrating. He wasn't always sure which lesson was which. So he often ate the clothes during Dressing Up, thinking it was Table Manners, during which he once did a poo on a plate because he thought it was Toilet Training.

The two nervous racehorses, Gangster's Moll and Minty Boy, took a while to settle in, and would jump and shriek at any loud noises and then gallop around, banging into things, trying to find somewhere to hide. The TV was smashed on day two of their arrival and three of Mrs Bold's favourite ornaments were knocked off the mantelpiece by a swishing tail. They could both be easily spooked and suffered from daily panic attacks. But there was no denying their determination to succeed, and they announced during Careers Advice that they wished to work as beauty therapists, and dreamed one day of starting their own salon.

Group Therapy proved to be a vital part of their rehabilitation and recovery. With quivering voices they managed to tell everyone about some of the horrible treatment they had suffered at the hands of their previous owner, Tarquin Twit-Twot.

'Awful as it was, that is all in the past,' Mr McNumpty told them. 'Try to let it go. You're amongst friends now.'

'Yes, you are,' confirmed Betty. 'We will never let anything nasty happen to you again.'

'Thank you,' said Minty Boy softly.

'Do you promise?' asked Gangster's Moll.

'Yes, we promise with all our hearts,' Bobby reassured them.

'Group hug, everyone!' cried Uncle Tony. And all the animals, of all shapes and sizes, gathered around the two frightened horses and gave them a long, tight hug, which made them feel much, much better.

So, day by day, week by week, the lessons

continued. To reassure Gangster's Moll and
Minty Boy that they were safe and no one was
still hunting for them, Miranda the marmoset
monkey still spent most of her time on the
lounge windowsill, watching out for anything
suspicious. 'I keep looky-eye out,' she told
the horses.

But there was no sign of any horseboxes, or indeed of Dodgy Dean. Fairfield Road remained a quiet, suburban street, where very little happened that was out of the ordinary.

For now, anyway.

Chapter

Every day, as usual, Betty and Bobby Bold went to school but were always home in time for the Group Therapy sessions, which they didn't take very seriously at all. In fact, the whole house seemed to be far too serious these days for the twins' liking and they missed all the laughter there used to be at Number 41. Well, they were hyenas after all.

One hot day in June they brought their best friend, Minnie, home for tea. She'd been desperate for weeks to meet the new Bold housemates and see the new Bold school she'd heard so much about from the twins. Mrs Bold had finally agreed to let her come but had warned Sheila to be on her best behaviour.

Perhaps someone should have warned the twins and Minnie to be on their best behaviour too, because once those children were together there was always going to be some trouble and mischief. And today was no exception.

When the children got home from school, as usual they found all the animals in the middle of a group therapy session in the lounge, and Minnie was soon very bored. 'I wish we could stop the session so I could meet everyone properly,' she said. 'That poodle looks hilarious. I love her outfit.'

Bobby started to giggle. 'I think I might have a brilliant idea,' he said, and producing a whoopee cushion, he crept into the lounge.

Roger was standing up addressing the group about his fear of open fields, so Bobby snuck up behind him and placed the whoopee cushion on the sheep's chair just before he sat back down. The loud farting noise which followed made everyone laugh, but unfortunately had the opposite effect on Gangster's Moll and Minty Boy, who flew into one of their tizzies and ran, whinnying, in circles.

To calm themselves down they stuck their heads and necks out of the window to get some air. But unfortunately the local Teddington police car was patrolling down Fairfield Road just at that moment, and the police officers' suspicions were quickly aroused.

'Hold up,' said Police Constable Pete, sitting in the front passenger seat. 'That seems odd, Bernard. I swear I just saw two horses hanging out that window.'

'Did you really? How very odd. Should I put the siren on?' asked PC Bernard, pulling gently up to the kerb outside 41 Fairfield Road.

'No, Bernie, not yet,' said Pete. 'Wasn't there something on the news about two runaway horses around here?'

'You're right, Pete!' exclaimed Bernard, narrowing his eyes. 'I think perhaps we should pay this residence a visit, pronto.'

'Gotcha,' said Pete as Bernard pulled the handbrake on and turned off the engine. 'There had better be a good explanation for this, or they're nicked.'

'Do we need our tasers or truncheons?' continued Pete, opening his door and getting ready to jump out.

'Both,' answered Bernard, his expression one of grim determination. 'This could be just the case we've been waiting for, Pete. "MISSING RACEHORSES FOUND IN TEDDINGTON SEMI." Imagine! We'll get an award, medals, promotion . . . maybe invited to tea at Buckingham Palace . . .'

Miranda, who had been dozing at her post on the windowsill, woke up when she heard the car doors slam and the policemen striding towards the house. She slipped off the sill to raise the alarm, crying, 'Men comes, men comes! Hide!' By then the horses had darted inside as quickly as they could, closed the window and drawn the curtains.

'Police!' whinnied Minty Boy. 'Maybe they saw us!'

'Police!' shrieked Miranda simultaneously in her high-pitched voice. 'Parked outside! Mr Boldy! Mrs Boldy!'

'They're coming! Police raid! Help! Help!' joined in Gangster's Moll, hysterical now and running in circles with a sweating Minty Boy. The other animals scattered in all directions as they dived for cover to avoid the blur of hooves, fur and horsey breath that filled the room.

Then came a firm, official-sounding knock at the door, and everyone froze in shocked silence.

'Emergency Drill!' said Mr Bold in a very loud whisper. 'Don't panic, everyone! Emergency! Emergency! You know the drill! We've been rehearsing for just this moment for the last few weeks.'

Sheila, Fifi, Roger, Minty Boy, Gangster's Moll, Bobby, Betty, Minnie, Uncle Tony, Mr McNumpty, Miranda and Mrs Bold all stared at him in wide-eyed dread. The room was full of the sound of thoughtful breathing.

Then came another, louder knock. 'Police!' came a muffled call. 'Open up, please, or we'll have to break the door down with, er, something big and heavy . . . Police!'

Mrs Bold was the first to snap out of it. 'Action stations, everyone! Chop chop!' she said with authority. Suddenly all the animals sprang into life, remembering the Emergency Drill they had practised. 'Fred, you go and answer the door. Stall them for as long as you can, dear!' said Mrs Bold.

Mr Bold gave a final, nervous glance around the room. 'Good luck, all,' he said. 'And remember – we do this for animals everywhere!'

He hurried down the hallway, calling out as cheerfully as he could, 'One moment! Sorry to keep you!' He patted his forehead to check his bristly fringe was as neat as possible, and then arranged his face into a friendly smile. Finally he opened the door.

'Good evening, officers,' he said with exaggerated calmness. 'How can I help you two gentlemen?'

'We have reason to believe,' said PC Bernard, peering over Mr Bold's shoulder as if he expected to see something very large and unusual behind him, 'that, er, something suspicious might be going on here.'

'Suspicious, ossifer? I mean, officer?' said Mr Bold, the picture of innocence. 'Whatever do you mean?'

'Horses, sir,' said PC Pete. 'Missing horses, to be precise. My colleague and I were patrolling this street when I thought I saw, leaning out of your front window, what appeared to be two racehorses. Can you explain this, sir?'

'Horses?' laughed Mr Bold nervously. 'Neigh! – I mean, no! I've never heard such nonsense! This is an ordinary family home. Where on earth would we put two great big horses?'

'We'd like to come in and have a look around, nevertheless,' said PC Bernard.

'Of course,' trembled Fred. 'But how about a quick joke first?' He raised his voice to cover a flurry of activity from within.

'I don't think we have time for that now, if you don't mind,' said PC Pete suspiciously. 'This is a serious visit.'

'Oh, always time for a good joke, surely?' stalled Fred. 'I make my living writing Christmas cracker jokes. You really must hear some. Here goes!'

Why did the chicken cross the playground?

To get to the other SLIDE! (Ha, ha! Do you get it?)

Why do gorillas have such big fingers?

Because they have such big nostrils.

The two police officers were stony-faced.

'Well, how about this one?'

'Very amusing, I'm sure,' said PC Bernard, attempting to **push** past Mr Bold. 'But if you don't mind—'

But Fred wasn't finished yet.

'I must say, that one was rather good!' said PC Pete, breaking into a chuckle. 'Which reminds me . . .'

Mr Bold laughed as long and as loudly as he could. Shaking his head with mirth, he said, 'Oh, very good, officer. Bravo! I must remember that one, I really must. I shall put it into a Christmas cracker, if you don't mind.'

PC Pete looked thrilled.

'Anyway, sir,' said PC Bernard, rocking backwards and forwards on his heels with impatience. 'If you don't mind, may we come in now?'

Mr Bold glanced nervously towards the lounge door. 'Why yes, of course! You won't find anything illegal going on here, I can assure you. No horses, ponies, donkeys or mules under *this* roof. The very idea! Just one happy family.' He led the way along the corridor and into the lounge.

Inside was a perfect picture of domestic contentment. Mr McNumpty and Uncle Tony were sitting at a small table by the window playing dominoes, Mrs Bold was standing by the bookcase, busy with some ironing, and the twins and Minnie were sitting on the sofa doing

their homework, a cute doll
in a pram by their side.
The two policemen came
in and looked around.

'Evening, all,' said
PC Bernard. 'Sorry to
disturb you.'

'Oh, no bother,' said
Mrs Bold as she spread a
large sheet over the rather
wobbly ironing board. 'I
expect you're only doing
your job. I hoof – I mean
have just been doing a spot
of ironing.'

'Are you looking for bank
robbers?' asked Bobby as
the officers walked around

the room, and stood to admire the two large lamps either side of the fireplace.

'Lovely pair, aren't they?' said Mr McNumpty. 'Antiques. I believe they're from the Far East.'

'Humph,' said PC Bernard, moving in to take a closer look. He was about to step onto the fluffy apricot hearth rug when Minnie called out, 'STOP! You can't walk on the rug with your big policeman boots!'

PC Bernard stopped where he was and looked down at the rug. 'Beg pardon?' he said.

'It's, er, priceless, you see,' jumped in Uncle Tony.

'Very delicate weave from, er, Morocco.'

'Very nice, I'm sure,' said PC Pete. 'Went there once on holiday with the wife.'

After a few minutes of awkward silence during which the policemen continued to look around the room, even examining the ceiling, under the sofa and behind the curtains, they shrugged at each other.

'Oh well,' said PC Bernard. 'Everything seems to be in order in here – Pete, you check the rest of the house.'

'Right–o,' said Pete, who then disappeared for a few minutes to inspect the other rooms. 'No sightings of any horses to report, Bernard,' he said when he returned. 'Smells a bit feral up there, mind you,' he added. 'But no law against that.'

'That may be my wife's perfume. It's called "Animal Magic",' said Mr Bold in a moment of inspiration. 'Not to everyone's taste . . .'

The two policemen stared at Mrs Bold, who shrugged. 'According to the slogan it's designed to "bring out the beast in your man".' She smiled coyly at Mr Bold.

PC Pete coughed. 'Ahem. Guess we'll be off then. Although I'm sure . . .' He trailed off mid-sentence.

PC Bernard took over, sounding suddenly determined. 'Now look here,' he said to the room in general. 'If my colleague says he saw horses leaning out of the window of this room then he almost definitely did. Where did you put 'em, eh?'

Everyone looked at him in astonishment. Betty stifled a giggle.

'Horses, did you say?' asked Mrs Bold, sounding incredulous. 'That's hilarious! What a funny suggestion! I haven't seen any horses in here, have you, children? Tony? Mr McNumpty? Mr Bold?' Everyone shook their heads vigorously at the very idea of two horses being in a lounge.

'You should rein in your imagination a little,' said Mr McNumpty.

What's the difference between a horse and a duck?

One goes quick, the other goes quack!

'Ha ha ha!' laughed Mrs Bold, and everyone apart from the policemen joined in. The lamp to the left of the fireplace began to tremble a little, but Mr McNumpty jumped up and stood in front of it so the gentlemen of the law didn't notice.

'No, officers. No horses in this room of any kind. As you can see. I suggest you try Bushy Park. Might see some there if you're lucky.'

'Must have been a trick of the light, I suppose . . .' said PC Pete, losing interest in the missing horses and rather enjoying the jokes instead.

Or you could look in the horse-pital!

Everyone laughed long and loud at Mr Bold's joke, including the two police officers – who had a few more of their own.

Mr Bold ushered the two laughing policemen towards the front door, tears of mirth running down their cheeks. By the time they fell out the door a few seconds later, they were laughing so much they could hardly stand up.

'Goodbye, officers!' said Mr Bold happily, waving to Pete and Bernard as they drove off. 'Do drop in whenever you're galloping by, I mean passing by!'

He shut the door at last, and breathed a sigh of relief before hurrying back to the lounge.

'Phew, that was close! All clear, folks!' he said.

With a loud exhalation the two lamps either side of the fireplace began to move, then legs appeared and lifted off the lampshades to reveal Minty Boy and Gangster's Moll.

'I was so nervous it wouldn't work, but it did!' said Minty Boy, slipping back down onto all fours.

Mrs Bold whipped the sheet off the ironing board and there was Sheila, lying flat and still across Roger's back.

'I got cramp a couple of times, but managed to breathe through it! Good job the iron wasn't actually switched on,' Sheila said, sliding onto the floor. 'It was jolly hard work keeping stiff and still like that. Got any cheese I could eat?'

'I must say you are quite a heavy girl!' exclaimed Roger, rubbing his sore shoulders against the side of the sofa. 'Did someone say cheese?'

'Heavy?' said Sheila indignantly. 'I'm just big-boned, that's all.'

Suddenly the apricot rug sprang to life. 'Alors!' declared Fifi. 'I was almost trodden on!'

'I saved you!' said Minnie proudly.

'Merci, beaucoup! You deserve a little Camembert, perhaps?'

'Well done, EVERYONE!' said a beaming Mrs Bold. 'Our Emergency Drill worked like a dream, and I'm very proud of you all, each and every one of you.'

'Cheese on toast all round!' declared Mr Bold, and he went to the kitchen to prepare a well-deserved tea for all the hungry housemates.

Chapter 10

After their close shave with the police, all the animals took their lessons a lot more seriously. The sooner they could walk, talk and work as humans, the better: one slip-up by any one of them and the future of them all would be in jeopardy. The next time someone came knocking at their door they might not be so lucky. Everyone was focused and determined – everyone apart from Sheila.

'I've an awful feeling I've made a terrible mistake,' she said during Group Therapy one day. 'I love being a crocodile. I've realised that. It was living in the sewers underneath Teddington that I didn't like.'

'Oh dear,' said Mrs Bold. 'You mean you don't want to live as a human any more?'

'No. I don't. I can't be bothered with the dressing up and the table manners, the pleases and thank yous. I have the overwhelming urge to stalk my own prey, SNAP and gulp it down in one swallow. I can't help it! I've tried and tried to change, but I'm afraid it's impossible.' Tears began to roll down the crocodile's cheeks. 'But what can I do?' Sheila sobbed. 'I can't fit down the toilet any more, I've grown too much. And even if I could, life down there is terrible.'

'How about the River Thames? You could splash about in there, and there are lots of fish. I've seen them,' suggested Bobby.

'Too dangerous.' Mr McNumpty shook his head. 'Imagine the fuss if a croc was seen in the Thames! I'm afraid the police would be involved again and this time they'd shoot you.'

This only made Sheila cry even more. 'I'm trapped!' she wailed. 'Stuck in a world I don't want to be in. It's all a terrible, wretched mistake.'

There was silence for a while. No one in the group could think of any way out of Sheila's situation.

'Maybe you're just having a bad day?' said Betty brightly. 'It happens to me sometimes. Then I have a warm bath and go to sleep and in the morning I feel much better. I wonder what I was so miserable about.'

'*Oui, ma chérie*,' agreed Fifi. '*Moi aussi!*

Me too! I have the artistic temperament, but always the sadness passes finalement.'

Uncle Tony passed the box of tissues that they always kept handy during Group Therapy, and Sheila wiped her big, green eyes.

'Yes, I expect you are right,' she said, not very convincingly. 'I'll feel better tomorrow, I'm sure.'

'This process isn't easy,' said Mrs Bold. 'But we are all here to support each other through the hard times as well as the good times. Would you like to try on one of my new hats? I've made one out of an old dustbin lid and some clingfilm. I think it will suit you.'

'Oh, Amelia,' said Sheila, brightening up at the thought. 'I don't mind if I do!'

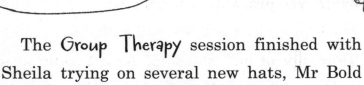

The Group Therapy session finished with
Sheila trying on several new hats, Mr Bold

telling lots of jokes and Fifi singing some cheerful songs. By the end of the hour Sheila was feeling a bit better, and she even announced that her desire to live as a crocodile again was probably just a phase.

'How silly of me!' she said. 'As if I could ever go back. I'd miss all of my friends here far too much for starters.'

Fifi meanwhile had a very different problem. As we have seen, she was excellent in all her classes, and while she looked marvellous in shimmering frocks and sequined skirts, she had to be gently informed that some daywear choices were also important.

'You can't walk down to the shops in THAT!' giggled Bobby. 'You'll stop the traffic!'

'But I am an artiste extraordinaire,' drawled Fifi, a little pompously. 'I like very much to stop the traffic. I feed off the attention.'

'But I thought we were trying to fit in, not stick out?' said Gangster's Moll, frowning.

'Speak for yourself!' answered Fifi.

She also made it very clear during Careers Advice that she was a singer who wanted to sing, and she would not be seeking any temporary jobs in the local supermarket or coffee shop. She refused to go to the Job Centre and insisted that Mr Bold find her some auditions instead.

'I am ready, I tell you. Prête! I have the dress, now I need an orchestra, make-up artist, hairdresser, manager and an audience! I must sing! C'est l'amour de ma vie!'

'It is very good to be confident, of course,' said Mr Bold, getting a little agitated. 'But you haven't even walked down Fairfield Road dressed as a human yet. You can't run before you can walk. Besides, we really can't afford an orchestra. Or any of those things. It's out of the question. You can't just suddenly become a star, you know. I believe, in show business, you have to start at the bottom.'

'Bottom?' repeated Fifi, her nose twitching. 'I know all about the bottoms. I am a chien, a dog, remember!'

'I have an idea,' piped up Minnie, who was visiting for the first time since the incident with the police. She was fascinated by show business and red carpets and thought Fifi was the most incredible creature she'd ever met. She was desperate to help her.

'What's that, dear?' asked Mrs Bold. Minnie always had very good ideas – although some of them could be a bit naughty.

'Well, our music teacher at school, Mr Trumpet, gives singing lessons in his spare time. He could teach Fifi, I'm sure. He wouldn't charge much, probably nothing, if I explain about my very talented but very poor friend who is visiting from France . . .' As she said this, Minnie put her arm affectionately around Fifi, who couldn't resist a quick lick of Minnie's cheek at the mention of her talent.

'Great idea, Minnie!' said Mrs Bold, clapping with joy.

'Oh, merci beaucoup! Thank you!' said Fifi, whimpering with excitement.

'I'll ask him tomorrow, then!' said Minnie.

'Yes. I think you're more than ready to go out and about as a human, Fifi dear. But don't lick the teacher,' cautioned Mrs Bold. 'He might not like it. And try not to chase your tail or growl. And if you accidentally do, just explain that you're French. Such things are traditional in your country.'

'Of course,' said Fifi dreamily. She was gazing into the distance now, imagining herself in front of a huge, adoring audience, all applauding wildly and calling 'Encore!'

'It's all very well,' said Mr McNumpty to Uncle Tony that evening as they played their usual game of dominoes before bedtime. 'Fifi is more than ready for her first trip on the outside. But everyone else is starting to feel a little cooped up. Stir crazy. Sheila's getting very snappy. I think if Fifi goes off for singing lessons it might cause jealousy, you know.'

'Oh no, we don't want that,' muttered Tony, remembering how exciting his own first outing had been, although he'd had to push Miranda around in the doll's pram, because he had trouble walking on his hind legs and needed something to prop himself up with.

'I'll have a word with Mr and Mrs Bold,' said Mr McNumpty decisively. 'Maybe there's somewhere we could all go. Just for a quiet stroll in the park, maybe. Get everyone out the house and stretching their legs.'

142

'What, all twelve of us?' asked Uncle Tony doubtfully, counting everyone up. 'Not including the cat or turtle or seagulls, I suppose, as they go out all the time anyway.'

'That's right. Everybody learning to pass as a human. And me, of course, making us twelve in total. It would be fun, wouldn't it? Might cheer Sheila up a bit too.'

'Mmm. If you're sure they are all ready.'

'There's only one way to find out . . . Your go,' replied Mr McNumpty.

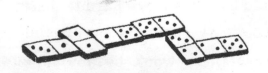

Chapter 11

As it happened there was a big fete in Bushy Park the following Sunday, with lots of attractions, including a Bouncy Castle, Tombola, Coconut Shy, Cake stall and a Fancy Dress parade with prizes.

After careful consideration Mr and Mrs Bold agreed with Mr McNumpty: a group outing would perk the whole household up and it was the perfect opportunity to try out the skills they had been trying so hard to master.

'I hope there won't be any slip-ups,' said Mrs Bold.

'Well, if there are we can say we all dressed up as animals as part of the Fancy Dress parade, can't we?' suggested Bobby.

'Perfect, son!' said Mr Bold, who made the announcement to the excited housemates after classes that day. Even the twins, Mr McNumpty and Uncle Tony, who were all used to going out and about, were thrilled at the prospect of going to the fete.

'Cake stall!' squealed Betty.

'Candyfloss!' cried Mr McNumpty.

'Toffee apples!' said Tony, licking his lips.

On the day of the fete, the excitement was at fever pitch in the two semi-detached houses in Fairfield Road. It was a lovely, bright, sunny day, perfect for the event in the park. The Bolds all wore their Sunday best, Mr McNumpty wore a light summer suit and Miranda a pretty floral doll's dress that fitted her perfectly. Tony didn't like dressing up and refused to wear anything other than his usual faded green tracksuit.

It was decided that to be on the safe side, the others – who were all about to take their very first steps out onto the streets of Teddington – should do a rehearsal before leaving, in front of the more experienced animals, just in case there were any glaring mistakes or giveaways, both in terms of dress and walking human-style. The Bolds, Mr McNumpty, Uncle Tony and Miranda sat in the lounge to watch the parade.

'Ready for the inspection!' called Mr Bold, and one by one the nervous recent arrivals came in, dressed up and walking unsteadily on their hind legs.

Sheila was wearing a long, dark green velvet skirt (to match her eyes), which hid her thick tail very nicely, a faded white cheesecloth blouse covered in a Spanish shawl decorated with roses, and on her head was a large-brimmed, floppy black sun hat. Her walk was a bit of a waddle, but as long as she didn't try to go too fast, not too distracting.

'Very good, Sheila!' exclaimed Mrs Bold. 'Your lovely eyes, though, are a little bit mesmerising . . . Maybe some large sunglasses?' Sheila nodded and went back to the dressing-up box to find some suitable ones.

Fifi was next. She had opted for a pink sequined crop top with matching lycra mini skirt revealing her long, shaved legs. She had backbrushed the fur on top of her head and ears into a big, shimmering pom-pom. She was wearing bright red lipstick, blusher and false eyelashes and carried a small white patent shoulder bag. She tottered in on a pair of rather high, white calf-length stiletto boots.

'Phwooaar!' said Mr Bold and he gave a wolf whistle.

'Oh dear,' stammered Mrs Bold, giving her husband a disapproving glare. 'Very, er, pretty, Fifi, but I'm not sure you should go out like that. People might think . . . How shall I phrase it?'

'I cannot help it if I am beautiful,' shrugged Fifi. 'Let them stare all they want. One day they will pay to look at me!' There was obviously no arguing with Fifi, so Mrs Bold just sighed and turned her attention to the rest of the animals.

Roger had opted for a wig of dreadlocks to cover his horns, and was wearing a rather fetching shirt undone almost to his navel.

'Blimey, Roger,' said Bobby. 'I didn't recognise you!'

But Roger had been as confused as usual and forgotten to put any trousers on.

'Really, Roger,' scolded Mrs Bold, 'we've talked about this before. You mustn't forget about your bottom half. You know how people talk.'

Roger looked a little tearful.

'Now now, don't upset yourself,' said Mrs Bold more kindly. 'Come upstairs after the dress rehearsal. I'll sort you out a pair of nice snug jeans. And I've got a rather fetching medallion somewhere which would set your woolly chest off a treat.'

Now it was the racehorses' turn to show their costumes. Standing on their back legs made Gangster's Moll and Minty Boy extraordinarily tall, but there was nothing much to be done about that. Their outfits, at least, were very credible. Both were dressed in matching grey dungarees over brushed-cotton gingham shirts. Their manes were worn forward, covering their large foreheads very well, and they each wore stylish cowboy hats and were chewing straw as they walked up and down in front of Mr and Mrs Bold's critical eyes.

'Bravo!' said Mr Bold. 'Very convincing indeed!'

'Like a couple of country bumpkins ready for a hoedown,' said Mrs Bold. 'Excellent!'

'Can we go to the fete now, please?' asked Bobby impatiently. He'd been looking forward to it for days and couldn't wait to join the fun.

'Yes, dear, in a moment,' said Mrs Bold, casting a final eye over everyone. 'Dad is just going to give a little pep talk, and then we shall be on our way.' She nudged Mr Bold, who stood up and cleared his throat.

'Right then, folks,' he began. 'Ready to go to the fete?'

There was a cheer from everyone, followed by a nervous whinny from Minty Boy.

'Just a few important things to remember . . . Number one, keep upright on your hind legs at all times. If you slip onto all fours, then pretend that you've dropped something and get back up as soon as you can. Number two, no animal noises, please. It will alarm the humans and draw attention to us. If you accidentally growl, BARK, neigh or snap, then try to make it sound as if you're having a bit of a cough, and say something like, "Goodness me, I do beg your pardon."

'Number three, stick together! It's a big park and there will be lots of people there, so don't wander off and get lost. If some of us want to go on one of the rides or try our luck on a stall, then the rest of us will stay and watch.

153

'Finally number four, and this is the most important: HAVE FUN!! Fetes are wonderful places and everyone will be happy and smiling and laughing. Especially us lot! READY? STEADY? LET'S GO!'

And so the unusual group stepped out of the front door of 41 Fairfield Road, one after the other, and tottered along the pavement towards the park.

Chapter 12

Mr Bold led the way to the fete, followed by Fifi and Sheila, who strolled arm in arm, breathing in the fresh summer air and looking about excitedly. Mrs Bold and the twins walked either side of Gangster's Moll and Minty Boy, who were quivering with nerves for the first few minutes in the outside world. Mr McNumpty sauntered behind with Uncle Tony, who pushed Miranda in her pram. Roger – his nether regions now covered by jeans – was by his side.

An elderly lady with a small yapping dog was the first person they encountered.

'Morning!' said Mr Bold cheerily.

'Lovely day,' she murmured, her eyes wide with surprise at the strange posse passing her by. The little dog pulled on his lead, trying to get a sniff of Fifi's bottom.

'Now now, Tiddles,' said the old lady.

'Ooh la la!' said Fifi, skipping to one side to avoid the little chap's twitching wet nose, but he began to bark excitedly. Sheila leaned towards him, lowered her sunglasses, and fixed the little pup with her hungry stare. That soon put a stop to his curiosity. He not only backed off, but jumped into his owner's arms with a high-pitched yelp.

As they got nearer to the park they could hear the sound of music, and the excited chatter and whoops of people enjoying themselves.

There were streams of revellers heading towards the gates to the fete. There were a few titters and stares, but as quite a lot of humans were in fancy dress, the Bold party felt as if they were blending in fairly well. In fact, some of the younger ladies at the fair seemed to be particularly impressed by Roger and his outfit and there were some admiring glances and nervous giggling when he walked past.

'Are you two OK?' Mrs Bold whispered to Minty Boy and Gangster's Moll as they entered the park. They'd gone very quiet all of a sudden.

'I'm bearing up,' said Minty Boy. 'I'm fighting the urge to bolt. But I must say it's rather thrilling to be out in the open after all this time.'

'Oh, doesn't that freshly cut grass smell divine?' said Gangster's Moll, and her large nostrils opened as wide as walnuts as she breathed in the delicious scent.

'I know it's hard for you,' said Betty, 'but remember – don't give the game away and start eating it. Sensible humans never touch grass!'

The fete was in full swing, with throngs of happy families, children and teenagers all enjoying themselves at the stalls or on the rides. The Bold party weaved their way through the colourful crowds, taking in all the sights, sounds and smells.

First they all had a go on the Lucky Dip – well, all except Sheila, as her arms were too short to reach. But she did enjoy going on the Coconut Shy, where the residents of Number 41 won three coconuts between them. Sheila ate hers in one gulp, which caused a shocked gasp from the human woman standing next to her.

The twins and Miranda had a wonderful time jumping up and down on the Bouncy Castle, laughing and screaming – Miranda was very good at somersaults!

Mr McNumpty and Uncle Tony had excellent luck on the Tombola, winning a bottle of elderflower cordial and some lavender-scented talcum powder (which Tony immediately sprinkled down the front of his trousers as he was getting rather hot and was worried he might start smelling hyena-ish).

At the Face Painting stall, Minty Boy opted for a superhero eye mask and Gangster's Moll had pretty butterflies painted across her forehead and down one side of her neck, while Mr and Mrs Bold spent ages deciding which cake to choose at the Cake stall and in the end plumped for a chocolate log and some macaroons.

What sort of cake does a baker with a cold make?

A cough-ee cake!

All the animals were being very well behaved, remembering their lessons, walking and talking like humans, so they decided to stay a little longer. Minnie's dad, the butcher, was running a delicious hamburger stall so everyone agreed to have their lunch there. But there was some confusion about the lack of cutlery required when eating hamburgers and chips wrapped in paper, especially after all the hours the animals had spent mastering knives and forks.

'What a waste of time that was!' said Sheila as they watched hungry humans eating with their fingers, no cutlery in sight.

'Ah, well,' explained Mr Bold. 'Sometimes they do that – but if you were in a restaurant you'd be asked to leave if you didn't use a knife and fork.'

'Most confusing!' muttered Sheila.

Fifi then gave a shriek of dismay when she saw a Hot Dog stall, and it had to be explained to her that hot dogs weren't actually dogs at all, just sausages in a roll.

'I will not eat one, on principle!' she said suspiciously. 'Quel bad taste!'

Apart from these moments of confusion, everyone was having a wonderful, relaxed afternoon, and the outing seemed to be a great success.

'Can we do this again soon, Dad?' said Bobby.

'I expect so, son. But I just saw you rubbing your bottom on that tree. That's not a very good example to set the others. Remember, when we're in public we have to behave like human beings.' Fred smiled as he said this though; he was actually rather proud of his son's bottom rubbing.

'Sorry, Dad!'

'Now, who'd like some candyfloss?' asked Mrs Bold a few minutes later, and she received an enthusiastic response from everyone.

The candyfloss stall was at the far side of the fete and the group set off happily. They were almost there when Minty Boy and Gangster's Moll suddenly stopped in their tracks, causing Mr McNumpty to bump into them and drop his elderflower cordial.

'Tsk!' he said, bending down to retrieve it, but he quickly realised that both horses were trembling from head to foot. 'What is it, Minty? Molly? Wassup?' he asked, but the two horses were frozen to the spot. Underneath their painted faces, Mr McNumpty could see the terror in their eyes.

Aware that the group was no longer all together, Mr and Mrs Bold stopped walking and turned back to see where the rest of them were. 'Something is wrong,' said Mr Bold. He then looked ahead to see what had spooked the horses. 'Oh dear,' he said. 'That explains it.'

To the right of the candyfloss stall, about twenty metres from where they were standing, was a large sign that said: 'PONY RIDES £2'. A sad and rather dirty-looking Shetland pony was carrying a child on his back and being led up and down a small enclosure by a gruff-looking man. The grass beneath his hooves was worn to dust where he had been traipsing endlessly up and down in the sun all afternoon.

'Poor thing!' declared Mrs Bold. 'About turn, everyone, let's forget about the candyfloss and have some toffee apples instead. Gangster's Moll and Minty Boy don't want to look at that poor pony, and I don't blame them.'

But Gangster's Moll and Minty Boy seemed unable to move.

'Upsetting for you, isn't it?' said Sheila sympathetically. 'Seeing one of your own kind looking so unhappy? I saw a woman just now with a crocodile handbag. Imagine how that made me feel! But there's nothing we can do about it at the moment, and you mustn't let it ruin your afternoon.'

'Mais, non,' said Fifi, looking from Minty and Molly to the pony and back again. 'It is something else. Why are they so terrified? I have the bad feeling. Le mauvais pressentiment!'

Suddenly Moll's agitation erupted and she simultaneously went down onto all fours and began to paw at the ground while shaking her head up and down with such force that her hat flew up in the air. 'NEEEEIGHH!' she cried.

'Uh-oh,' said Miranda, jumping from her pram to retrieve the hat.

Moll's behaviour set off Minty Boy, who whinnied loudly then pawed the air with his front hooves, snorting and pulling his lips back to reveal his very horse-like teeth.

'Steady on, Minty, old boy!' said Uncle Tony. 'Try to stay calm! You'll give the game away.'

'Mummy, look!' cried a little boy who was in the candyfloss queue. 'Why are those people acting like that?'

'I don't know, dear,' answered his mother, looking warily over. 'But try not to stare. I expect they aren't feeling too well.'

Mrs Bold was scared now – it looked very much as if Minty Boy and Gangster's Moll were about to lose control completely and revert to racehorse behaviour in public. If they started galloping around the fete in a panic, then the incident would quickly become not only out of control but also dangerous: children and adults might be trampled or accidentally kicked – to say nothing of the whole household's cover being blown. People were already starting to stare and back away.

'Deep breaths, Molly,' said Mr Bold desperately. 'Hold it together, both of you, please!'

'I – I – can't!' said Minty Boy. 'It's not the pony, it's . . . the MAN looking after them!'

'Who, dear?' asked Mrs Bold, turning to have a look. By now the man's attention had been drawn to the Bolds' posse. He abandoned the pony and walked towards them, grim-faced, carrying a rope.

'You don't understand,' trembled Gangster's Moll. 'It's DODGY DEAN . . . and I think he's spotted us!'

By now both horses were on all fours and had lost their cowboy hats. The dungarees, gingham shirts and face paint did little to hide the truth, unfortunately.

'Well I never,' growled Dodgy Dean, a thick-set man with missing teeth, a scraggly beard and fuzzy hair tied in a greasy ponytail at the back of his head. 'If it isn't our two runaways! Thought you'd given me the slip, did ya?' he said, roughly pushing poor Tony and the twins out of his way. 'Stand back, please, folks!'

'I'm sorry, everyone,' said Minty Boy hurriedly, 'but we're going to have to run for it!' Just as Dean was reaching out to grab them, the two horses whinnied a fierce battle cry, reared up once, then leaped in the air, right over Dean's head. Parents pulled their children out of the horses' path, women screamed and men SHOUTED as Minty and Molly broke into a gallop. Clods of earth flew up in the air behind them and into the eyes of Dodgy Dean, who was in hot pursuit.

'Come 'ere, you wretched beasts!'

In the chaos that ensued, Mr McNumpty urgently insisted that the rest of the party hurry home to safety before anyone put two and two together and realised this was not a group of humans.

'I'll stay here and see if I can help Molly and Minty escape, or maybe track them down once they've got away. I've got the nose for it,' he said urgently, tapping the side of his powerful bear snout. 'Who knows how this is all going to end.'

'Thank you, Nigel,' said Mr Bold. 'Fifi, Roger, Sheila – you get yourselves home with us. Quick, now! This is no place for you.'

Police sirens could be heard in the distance and a man was shouting through the loudspeaker for everyone to stay out of the way of the two rampaging horses wearing dungarees. There was crying and chaos in all directions. The thunderous noise of Molly and Minty's galloping hooves echoed around the fete and the two thoroughbreds could just about be seen through a cloud of dusty earth, racing around the perimeter of the high fence enclosure, obviously in too much of a panic to find their way out. Shocked and shaken families were running out of the gate in droves.

'I thought those two didn't like running,' said Bobby. 'They're certainly making up for it now.'

'Maybe they just don't like running with a jockey on their back,' suggested Betty.

'Hurry, kids! Let's go,' cried Mrs Bold. 'We can't help here. Let's get back to safety!'

Mr McNumpty promised he'd let everyone

know what was going on as soon as possible, and Mr and Mrs Bold ushered their frightened party out of the park and along Fairfield Road to Number 41.

Fifi was almost overcome with the afternoon's drama. As soon as they got home she flopped on the sofa with a cologne-soaked muslin cloth covering her eyes, and Betty fanned her with a copy of *Vogue* magazine.

Sheila had a long soak in the bath. As she lay there in the warm, fragrant bubbles she thought what a shame it was that she wasn't allowed to deal with Dodgy Dean in the way a wild crocodile would have. 'SNAP, SNAP, swallow!' she thought to herself. 'Problem solved.'

Roger was sitting alone in Mr McNumpty's back bedroom, feeling very confused. During all the chaos, a lady from the Coconut Shy had slipped him a piece of paper with her phone number on and given him a wink. But he didn't have a phone to call her with, and even if he had he couldn't understand what she wanted to speak to him about. So in the end he decided to just eat the piece of paper.

Chapter

13

Back at the park after half an hour of chasing and hollering, Dodgy Dean had finally managed to corner the exhausted and terrified Minty and Molly between the fence and the Coconut Shy. The two horses hated running, and they'd had enough and had to give in.

'Gotcha!' spat Dean triumphantly. He tied his rope into a lasso, looped it over the poor horses' heads and pulled them roughly back towards the yellow horsebox, the very one they had escaped from several weeks before. Their human clothes had flown off in the chase and they walked with bowed heads, sweating and panting, their muscles quivering from all the excercise.

'This is it, my dear friend,' whispered Gangster's Moll to Minty.

'Yes, Sweet Moll,' said Minty Boy softly. 'There's no escape now, for sure.'

The two walked meekly into the filthy horsebox. There was no point in resisting any more. It was all over.

'Weird, innit, how you two turned up at a fete in Teddington, wearing dungarees and cowboy hats?' Dean laughed at them as he secured the door. 'I'm not taking any chances with you this time. Straight to the slaughterhouse for you two. You won't be able to run away once you're dead.'

And because Molly and Minty had escaped before, Dean decided to not only double-lock the horsebox but to fix the steel bar across it and add chains and padlocks, just to be sure.

Molly and Minty had been in the darkened box for several minutes before they realised that the poor bedraggled pony was locked in with them too.

He was so tired after his day's work that he could barely keep his eyes open.

'Afternoon,' he said sadly, with a Scottish accent. 'My name is Hamish. Count yourselves lucky. The slaughterhouse is better than the life I live, I promise you.' And then he fell into an exhausted sleep as Dodgy Dean got into the cab of the horsebox and began to drive away.

Chapter

14

No one felt like going to bed that night in the Bold household. They were all too concerned about their friends. They gathered in the lounge to fret and worry together. But slowly, as the hours passed, one by one they all fell into a troubled sleep.

It was gone midnight when a breathless Mr McNumpty tapped on the front door. Mr Bold opened it and the grizzly bear staggered in, asking for water.

'Wake up, everyone,' said Mr Bold. 'Nigel's

back, and hopefully he has some news. Make some space for him on the sofa.'

They all gathered around Mr McNumpty anxiously.

'Well,' he began, after gulping down the water and catching his breath a little. He looked very tired and windswept. 'I'm afraid it isn't good news. Minty and Molly have been captured by that ruffian. I know I'm a bear and I should have got my teeth and claws out to save them, but the police were watching. They'd have shot me on the spot if they had known I was a grizzly bear.'

Mrs Bold patted his shoulder kindly.

'And what has Dodgy Dean done with them?' asked Roger.

'He's locked and bolted them in the horsebox – I found an abandoned bicycle in a hedge at the fete and borrowed it. Luckily the horsebox is such a battered old banger it couldn't go very fast. I managed to follow them all the way to the abattoir in Hayes. Dodgy Dean is parked outside, guarding them until morning. My poor legs have never worked so hard!'

'Non!' gasped Fifi, pressing a silk handkerchief to her forehead as if she were about to faint.

'What's an abattoir?' asked the twins.

'Er, it's . . . not a very nice place for animals,' said Mrs Bold.

'But what is it?'

'You know how you see animals in the fields,

running about?' said their mother.

'Yes,' nodded the twins in unison.

'Then you see meat in the butcher's or on the shelves in the supermarket? All packed up neatly?'

'Yes,' said the twins again. 'We've been to Minnie's house – her dad's a butcher.'

'Well, an abattoir is the process by which that happens.'

'Or to put it another way, my dears,' explained Sheila, drawing a green claw across her throat, 'goodbye to Minty Boy and Gangster's Moll, and hello to horse steaks . . .'

'Argh!' said Betty. 'They've been killed?'

'Got it in one,' said Sheila. 'Taken there and—'

'Well, not quite yet!' interrupted Mr McNumpty. 'But they will be if we can't get them out of there before dawn when the abattoir opens. We need a plan of action – and fast!'

'Thinking caps on, everyone!' said Mr Bold.

But for a long time there was only silence in the room.

'The trouble is,' said Roger, sounding very concerned, 'we are all animals. For us to go anywhere near an abattoir is madness, surely?'

'You mean we get "processed" too?' squeaked Miranda.

Roger nodded solemnly. 'Especially me. I've

seen fields full of sheep driven off in the past. And they never come home again.'

'Our poor friends!' wailed Fifi. 'Quelle horreur!'

'This is no time to be sheepish and timid,' said Mr Bold firmly. 'We need to be brave and determined. This is a life or death situation.'

'We've *got* to get there and rescue them!' said Bobby, jumping up and punching the air. 'Show that nasty Dean what happens when he messes with us Bolds!'

'That's my boy!' said Mrs Bold, patting him affectionately on the back. 'Come on, everyone. Be positive!'

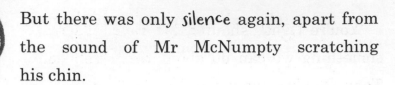

But there was only silence again, apart from the sound of Mr McNumpty scratching his chin.

Uncle Tony was sitting thoughtfully in his armchair when he stood up and cleared his throat. 'There must be something,' he said. Everyone turned to look expectantly at him. 'Well, er, give me a moment. Look at the skills we have between us: we've got a crocodile who SNAPS, a poodle who sings, a grizzly bear who can bite and scratch, hyenas who can dig, a sheep with horns, a monkey who can do acrobatics – not to mention flying, squawking seagulls. And what has stupid Dodgy Dean got?'

'Er, the keys to the padlocks?' said Roger.

'Apart from that, then?' continued Uncle Tony.

'You're right!' shouted Mr Bold. 'There IS something we can do about this! Well done, Tony. You've given me an idea! I'm such a clever hyena, I really am! Bobby and Betty, go and grab a couple of blankets and some ropes. Everybody else, in the car at once. I'll tell you my plan as we drive to Hayes. And we won't need any human clothes for this,' he said, starting to take off his pyjamas. 'We shall do this au naturel. It's our animal skills that will save the day! Bobby, can you quickly lean out the window and call the seagulls, tell them to follow us? We'll be needing all the help we can get.

'Pay attention, everyone, we will only have one chance at this. But if it works we should ALL be back here in time for breakfast – including Minty Boy and Gangster's Moll!

'One last thing . . .'

Chapter

So what was this plan? Well, if I tell you it will spoil the surprise. But take it from me, Mr Bold is as clever as he thinks he is – and rescuing animals is what he's good at. So it's a great plan. Fingers crossed it works!

It was a tight squeeze in the car that night as they drove through the deserted streets towards Hayes. Mr Bold was driving and Mrs Bold sat in the front seat with Miranda on her lap. Fifi (much to her horror) sat in the middle in the back, sandwiched between Sheila and Roger, who had the twins perched on their laps. Mr McNumpty led the way on the 'borrowed' bicycle with Uncle Tony perched on the crossbar. Far above them the seagulls glided through the night sky. They flew in a V formation, calling out 'V for victory! V for victory!' as they went.

Mr McNumpty stopped in a quiet street about half a mile from the abattoir. 'I think we should walk from here,' he said. 'It's not too far and we want to surprise Dodgy Dean.'

The seagulls perched on a fence and everyone gathered around Mr Bold as he whispered his master plan to them.

'Everything must happen just as I say, understand? It's the only way it will succeed! We must work together. Tally ho!'

They all had a part to play in the daring

rescue attempt, and as they walked towards their destination the group was very quiet as they thought about their roles.

A few minutes later they turned a corner into an industrial estate.

'There's the horsebox!' whispered Mr McNumpty, pointing to a large yellow vehicle glowing in the moonlight about a hundred metres ahead. It was parked beside a set of ominous metal gates and a sign that read 'HAYES ABATTOIR'. In a few hours those gates would open, and clearly Dean intended to be first in the queue . . . Those pesky horses had escaped once before and he didn't want to take any chances this time. They would fetch him a good price!

'Right,' breathed Mr Bold. 'Operation Rescue is about to be activated! Miranda? Seagulls? Stand by! We only have one stab at this, everyone, so good luck to all. And remember: BE BOLD!'

The first part of the plan was for the seagulls to glide around the horsebox and see if Dean was in there. He was snoring soundly in the cab, several empty cans of cheap lager propped on the dashboard.

'In a drunken stupor!' reported the seagulls.

'Excellent!' said Mr Bold with determination. 'Onwards with the next stage!'

Inside the horsebox Minty and Molly were nuzzling each other sorrowfully. They hadn't been able to sleep a wink, partly because of Hamish's snoring but also because they knew the fate that awaited them.

'I was so looking forward to our new life!' sighed Molly, a big horsey tear rolling down her cheek.

'Me too,' said Minty. 'We were doing so well too, thanks to the kindness of the Bolds. But now look at us! Dirty, thirsty, HUNGRY and locked up!'

'And very soon . . .' said Molly, a lump rising in her throat. 'We'll be—'

'It'll all be over very quickly,' said Hamish, who had just woken up. 'I feel so sorry for you though. Beautiful horses like you deserve a better life. Unlike mine . . .'

But just then they heard a very faint tapping on the door.

'Shsssh!' said Minty. 'What's that noise?'

All three horses twitched their ears to listen intently. There it was again. Tap, tap, tappety-tap!

'They're coming for us!' said Molly, starting to quiver.

'Who are?' asked Hamish fearfully.

'It's time!' said Molly, beginning to shake.

'Wait a sec,' said Minty. 'I think someone is trying to speak to us. Listen!' Straining to hear, they just about made out a few faint, high-pitched words, spoken in a voice so quiet no human would ever hear it.

'Minty! Molly! It's Miranda. You hear me?'

'Yes, yes, we can hear you!' said Molly.

'Who is Miranda?' asked Hamish.

'Our friend,' Molly explained quickly. 'Marmoset monkey.'

Hamish frowned. 'Aye, of course.'

'Listen carefully what I tell you,' continued the monkey urgently. 'We come rescue you. Keep still and calm until the doors are opened – then you must run. Fast. Faster than you ever run before. You understand? Back to Fairfield Road. The twins will go with you – they can follow their noses and show you the way home.'

'Oh, but that's so far and we're not very good at running,' explained Molly.

'You must!' said Miranda. 'It's your only hope.'

'Right,' nodded Minty Boy. 'We will have to, just this once.'

'Good,' said Miranda. 'Your lives depend on it.'

'But how will you ever get this door open?' worried Molly. 'Dean will never let us get away a second time – he's ruthless, he'll kill you!'

'No worry about a thing!' Miranda reassured her. 'Just stay calm and get ready to run like windy.'

'Another thing,' said Minty quickly. 'There are three of us in here. Hamish the pony is with us.'

'Er, no probs!' said Miranda. 'I'll go tell Mr and Mrs Boldy. More the merrier, I'm sure!'

Then there was calm for a moment while everyone got ready for the next part of the plan to begin.

'If we get out of here you're coming with us,' explained Molly to Hamish.

'But won't I slow you down?' asked Hamish, trying to keep up with the sudden events. 'I've got very short legs and they dinnae work terribly well.'

'Nonsense,' said Minty. 'You're one of us and we can't leave you behind to live a terrible life with that dreadful Dean man. I've no idea how they're going to try and get us out of here, but if they do, you're coming with us.'

'Thanks, pal,' said Hamish gratefully.

The seagulls circled above the horsebox for a few minutes until Mr Bold gave the signal. One by one, like planes coming into land, they swooped down and tapped their beaks noisily on the windscreen. Dodgy Dean awoke with a start.

'What the—?' said Dean, rubbing his head. 'Blighters – I'll soon show them.' He opened the van doors and got out, swiping at the air as the six seagulls continued to swoop and dive, leading him a few metres along the road. Dean snapped a thin branch from a nearby tree, then bashed and jabbed at his airborne assailants, shouting with anger and using some terrible words that I can't possibly write down. 'Bl***rgh!' he grunted. 'Little sl***#@$**s!' he roared.

Having got the man exactly where wanted him, the seagulls then unleashe secret weapon: poo. Splosh, splash, his eyes.

'Aarrgh!' cried Dean, droppi and covering his face. 'Stings He pulled a hanky from his to wipe the muck from his

made them sting more. And still the seagulls swooped, dropping more and more runny seagull poo on the dastardly man until it was all over his head and face.

By now Dean was rolling on the floor trying to cover himself.

'Go, Roger! Go, Fifi!' was the next order from Mr Bold.

Roger charged, head down and horns gleaming magnificently in the moonlight, towards the pitiful figure, crashing into him and causing more 'Oofs!' and 'Aarghs!' Roger backed away a little, pawed the ground and charged again.

Already blinded by the seagull poo, the bewildered man didn't know what on earth was attacking him now, and he cried with fear.

Just then Fifi joined the fray, growling and howling as she circled him and giving the occasional nip for good measure whilst Roger ran around him in circles, snorting loudly and nudging with his horns whenever Dodgy Dean looked like he might be attempting to stand up.

'Werewolves!' trembled Dodgy Dean. 'I'm going to be eaten alive!' And he sobbed even harder.

'Go, Bobby! Go, Betty!' called Mr Bold, and the twins ran into the scene eager to do their part. They too circled Dean, but unfurling ropes as they went so he was soon tied up and unable to see or move.

'Tony? Mr McNumpty? Go shut 'im up!' was Mr Bold's next order. The two older members of the Bold household trotted over now and put a stop to the noise by tying some old socks and underpants around the mouth of the noisy horse thief. Finally he was unable to see, move or speak.

'Well done, you lot!' cried Mr Bold, very pleased with the rescue mission so far. But they still had to get into the horsebox and release Minty and Molly.

'Amelia, could you go and get the padlock keys from the cabin?' asked Mr Bold urgently.

'Yes, dear,' answered Mrs Bold, heading determinedly towards the horsebox. She searched on the dashboard amongst the empty lager cans, in the cabinet and the van door compartments but found nothing.

'Oh dear,' she said. 'He must have the keys somewhere in his pocket.' She looked over at the horrid man writhing on the muddy roadside, covered in mess and trussed up with rope. 'I don't think I fancy rummaging through his pockets. Must I?'

'Won't hear of it, my dear!' said Mr Bold chivalrously. 'I would never put my own, dear wife through such an ordeal. Who needs keys when we've got Sheila?!' He gave Sheila a nod and she darted into action.

Much as she felt like slithering over to Dean and making a meal of him there and then, Sheila followed Mr Bold's orders and headed instead for the back of the horsebox. The chains were thick and rusty, but she pushed her lower jaw up against the van doors and wriggled until she had a good grip under the chains. She then took a deep breath and with as much force as she could muster she crashed her upper jaw downwards. Nothing happened with the first two bites, which made Sheila cross. The third, furious bite was a gigantic CRUNCH! that caused metallic sparks to fly up in the air. With a heavy clink the severed chains fell to the ground. Everyone applauded (apart from Dodgy Dean, who couldn't have even if he'd wanted to, which he wouldn't have, even though he couldn't).

Mr Bold bounded over to the back of the horsebox and, with Mr McNumpty's help, slid the heavy metal bar across and out. Still the door wouldn't open though. 'It's locked!' he cried.

'Pah!' said Sheila. 'I'm just getting the taste for this. Let me at it!' This time she used her smaller front teeth, gripping the rusty lock tightly and twisting her body. With a crunch of splintering wood she pulled the lock out of the door in one piece, then deftly spat it over her shoulder.

Finally, the doors swung open to reveal Minty Boy, Gangster's Moll and Hamish, all blinking at them.

'Oh, you've done it!' said a shaky Minty Boy as he climbed gingerly out of the horsebox and looked around.

'Thank you, thank you, everyone!' said Gangster's Moll, taking some deep breaths of fresh air and shaking her mane with delight. 'Come on, Hamish! I'll introduce you to everyone later.'

'Don't thank us yet, folks,' cautioned Mr Bold. 'It's not over until we are all safely home at Number 41. Bobby? Betty? Climb on Minty and Molly's backs – otherwise they'll look like runaways or won't know where to go – and get them home as fast as possible. I know you don't like running, you two, but I'm sure you can do it just this once, eh? And Miranda, you ride little Hamish.'

The three horses nodded eagerly in agreement.

Minty glanced up the road at Dodgy Dean. 'We know we're running away from him so it'll be easy. Hamish, you trot between us. Climb aboard, twins! See you back at the ranch, everyone.' And with a thankful bow, Minty and Molly cantered off through the industrial estate, Hamish hardly visible between them, the seagulls flying a little ahead of them, leading the way home.

For good measure Mr Bold and the others hauled Dodgy Dean to his feet and bundled him into the back of the horsebox before sliding the metal bar back into place and biting all the tyres so there was no chance he could follow them.

Dodgy Dean was so scared and bewildered he didn't utter a word. But just before they left the van to pile back into the car and drive home, they did hear a muffled 'Urgh!' from Dean.

'I think our friend might just have rolled in one of Minty Boy's rose garden specials,' said Mr Bold, and everyone laughed and cheered as they clambered back into the Honda.

Chapter 16

By the time the new day dawned everyone was gathered in the lounge at 41 Fairfield Road, tired but triumphant, enjoying a hearty breakfast. Hamish was introduced to all the residents and was beaming with delight at his new circumstances.

'This is all fantastic!' he sighed contentedly. 'After years of hard slog I've somehow landed on my hooves at last.'

'You deserve a good life after what you've put up with, Hamish,' said Uncle Tony.

'And can I really stay here?' asked the little Shetland.

'You are very welcome,' said Mr Bold kindly.

'I can't believe it's all over,' said an emotional Minty Boy with his mouth full of hay.

'Another hour or so and we'd have been driven through those gates to our doom!' shuddered Gangster's Moll. 'How can we ever thank you all enough?'

'You are a part of our family,' said Mr Bold, patting both horses affectionately on their shoulders as he tucked into a bacon sandwich. 'We all stand together.'

'We weren't going to let that tasty – I mean nasty – man get away with it,' added Sheila. 'Pass the tomato ketchup please, Fifi dear.'

'He'll think twice about taking any more horses to the abattoir now!' laughed Bobby.

'Yes, but I think it would be wise for us to lie low for a little while,' said Mr Bold. 'Particularly you horses. No more fetes or sticking your heads out the window for a while.'

After breakfast, the twins and Miranda gave all three horses a good wash and groom to clean away any trace of their terrible ordeal. Their manes were brushed too so they looked and felt much better.

'I had no idea I was so attractive under all the dirt!' said Hamish, admiring himself in a full-length mirror.

'I think we should all get some rest,' yawned Mrs Bold.

Did you hear about the man who plugged his electric blanket into the toaster?

He kept popping out of bed all night!

'I shall sleep like a log,' said Mrs Bold.

'Then you'll probably wake up in the fireplace!' said her husband.

One by one the housemates all slipped off to bed. Minty and Molly stayed where they were in the lounge and fell asleep standing up. Hamish lay on the sofa and had the best sleep he'd had for years.

Chapter

It was the middle of the afternoon by the time anyone stirred. And they were woken by the sound of Fifi running down the stairs in a panic.

'Alors!' she yelped. 'Quick! C'est aujourd'hui le jour! Today is the day! I almost forgot!'

'The day for what?' asked Mrs Bold, racing downstairs in her dressing gown.

'Vite!' said Fifi, hurriedly applying some lipstick. 'For my first singing lesson, that's what! I have to meet

222

Monsieur Trumpet in half an hour!'

'Ah, of course,' said Mrs Bold. 'I'll help you, don't worry.'

'Where is the pink chemisier? Et la jupe noire?' asked Fifi, throwing various items of clothing over her shoulder as she searched for the perfect blouse and skirt combination. 'This is it, Madame Bold,' she said portentously. 'My first step on the path to stardom! *Chanteuse extraordinaire!* La, la, la, la, laaaa!'

As it turned out, Mr Trumpet agreed with Fifi's assessment of her own talent. He thought she was a very good singer indeed. She could go far. The first lesson was a huge success, and

week after week he became more enthusiastic about Fifi's progress.

'You sing from the heart, Fifi,' he told her. 'And with such emotion! There is an animal quality to your voice which is quite extraordinary. Some notes you almost seem to howl!'

Everyone else, meanwhile, continued with their lessons at Number 41, with varying degrees of success. Roger's human speech was coming along really well. He loved playing with and looking after the twins, and his dream was still to work as a nanny one day. Every night he practised singing nursery rhymes, and of course his favourites were 'Baa Baa Black

Sheep' and 'Mary had a Little Lamb'. Eventually he started a part-time course in Childcare at Kingston College, and it began to look as if his dream might one day become a reality. (As long as he remembered to wear his trousers, of course. There had been an unfortunate incident in the supermarket recently.)

Molly and Minty took a while to recover from their traumatic adventure. It was some time before they ventured out again, and even then they looked nervously over their shoulders a lot, afraid that Dodgy Dean was going to pounce.

But eventually they stopped worrying. Dodgy Dean clearly knew when he was beaten and there was no trace of him. So, dressed up and walking on their hind legs, this tall and strikingly attractive pair became more confident. When they strolled down

Teddington High Street people still stared — but it was a stare of admiration, nothing more. In fact, a well-spoken young man in an orange Porsche drew alongside Molly one afternoon, introduced himself as 'Henry' and asked if he could take her out to a wine bar one evening. Molly batted her eyelashes and said thank you, but she didn't drink wine.

In the evenings, when the twins came home from school, often with Minnie in tow, Molly and Minty would set up their Beauty Salon in the kitchen and practise on the youngsters, styling Minnie's hair and make-up, painting Betty's nails or giving Bobby a relaxing head massage. Hamish — who couldn't yet walk on his hind legs, talk, use cutlery or the toilet, but was just happy to be away from Dodgy Dean's clutches — called himself their assistant, but really just stood around laughing at their efforts.

The trouble was, the word 'beauty' didn't really describe the results. The horses needed fingers, unfortunately – hooves just don't lend themselves to beauty treatments or massages: Minnie looked like a dog's dinner gone wrong, Betty had more nail polish up her legs than on her nails, and Bobby's head was so bruised after his 'massage' that he had to go and have a lie down in a darkened room.

'Oh dear,' said Molly one evening after it had all gone particularly wrong and Betty was scrubbing nail polish off her chin. 'I get the feeling we're not very good at this, Minty.'

'I agree, my dear,' said Minty Boy despondently. 'We're never going to be able to open our own salon, let's face it. What ARE we going to do with ourselves?'

'I think we need to have a good long think,'

concluded Molly. 'Let's go into the garden and have a nibble of the lawn.'

In fact, it was Bobby who came up with an idea for the two unemployed horses. He was feeling better after his rest that evening (although he was wearing sunglasses as he still had a bit of a headache).

'You need a job doing something you are good at,' he told the pair, who were still chewing grass thoughtfully in the back garden an hour later.

'That's the problem,' said Minty Boy. 'We don't seem to be gifted at anything in particular.'

'We are racehorses who don't like running. We're useless!' agreed Molly, returning from the flowerbed where she had deposited something to make the roses happy.

'That's it!' said Bobby suddenly as he watched the steam rising behind Molly.

'What's it?' asked Molly and Minty in unison.

'It's obvious when you think about it!' continued Bobby excitedly. 'Look at the lawn where you've been nibbling . . . perfect! And look how wonderful all our roses are thanks to your help. You should be gardeners! You can take care of people's lawns, eating a bit of grass when no one is watching, and with a wheelbarrow full of your special manure – and maybe a bit of Roger's if he's willing to part with it – your customers' flowers will all look spectacular!'

Molly and Minty nodded enthusiastically. 'Oh, well done, Bobby!' said Molly. 'We'll love being outside in the fresh air too. It's a fantastic idea. And Hamish can be our trainee!'

'Minty and Molly's Marvellous Garden Makeovers!' said Minty. 'We'll get some leaflets printed and post them through everyone's letterboxes. We'll be rushed off our hooves in no time. Hurrah for Bobby! That knock on the head seems to have done you the power of good!'

Unlike the others, however, Sheila wasn't making such good progress. She could talk human well enough, and walk upright when she could be bothered, but she just wasn't happy. She hated wearing clothes. They felt wrong on her skin. She liked to be wet and spent most of her day lolling in the bath, dreaming about swimming. She was always hungry too. Grateful as she was to Mr and Mrs Bold for letting her stay and for feeding her, the food they provided was just not enough for her. She had an overwhelming urge to chase and catch her own dinner: a packet of sausages and a couple of pork chops just didn't satisfy Sheila. And sometimes it took every inch of self-control not to gobble up the kittens or make a meal of Minnie. If she went out anywhere, it was to Teddington Lock to gaze at the water and imagine swimming around freely, snapping at the odd fish or (she daren't say it out loud) person.

But there was something else too. Sheila wanted to have children – baby crocodiles of her own. And that was never going to happen

233

if she lived her life as a human and didn't find a mate.

'Would you like to return to the sewers, then?' asked Mrs Bold during a Group Therapy session where Sheila had been particularly tearful.

'No! It was too awful down there,' cried Sheila. 'There is no mate for me amongst that smelly bask of crocs. And when I see you and your twins tickling and nibbling each other on grooming night, I long to have the same thing. I want little crocs of my own. I want to teach them how to swim and hunt, and how to clean their teeth. I can't possibly raise children down there.'

The reality was that no one could think of a solution. Sheila seemed trapped in her new life, and while all the others were enjoying themselves and working towards fulfilling their ambitions, Sheila couldn't see a way forward, backward or sideways. What on earth was she going to do?

Chapter
18

With Mr Trumpet's tuition, Fifi's singing was getting better and better. And one day the teacher announced that the talented poodle was ready to perform in front of the public.

'Look,' he said, pointing to an advert in the local paper. 'There is a talent competition at Teddington Town Hall in three weeks' time. I think you should enter!'

'Alors, and so my destiny, it begins,' said Fifi, misty-eyed.

She became very grand back at Fairfield

Road in the days before the competition, wafting about in a kimono and a feather boa.

'Miranda, ma chérie, a bowl – I mean a glass – of water for me, s'il vous plaît. *Je suis* parched.'

But everyone at Fairfield Road was very excited for Fifi and immediately booked front-row tickets for the night of the competition for themselves and Minnie. They listened to her rehearse her number for several hours each evening, until they all knew every note. Mrs Bold scoured the charity shops for a suitable dress, and found a full-length evening gown in black sequins with a matching beret. And Minnie helped Fifi find the perfect hairstyle.

Finally the big night arrived. The Bolds, Mr McNumpty, Tony and Miranda, Roger, Sheila, the horses and Minnie all put on their best clothes for the event. (Even the seagulls came along, flying up to the windowsill outside, their beaks pressed to the glass.) The town hall was packed to the rafters and the atmosphere was electric. Everyone from Numbers 39 and 41 Fairfield Road sat in the front row eating chocolates and clapping politely during the other acts – jugglers, dancers and comedians – but really they were waiting for Fifi to appear.

When she was finally introduced, Fifi sauntered into the spotlight and closed her eyes for a moment. The audience held their breath. Finally, when she was ready, she sang:

'Paris in the springtime
Is stunning, don't you think?
You can find true love there
And nice cheap plonk to drink.'

Her voice trembled with emotion, her dress sparkled under the lights and Fifi looked every inch a superstar.

Everyone was spellbound.

'Paris in the autumn,
Its charm just never fails
Romance is in the air
And for tea you can eat snails.'

When her song finished the applause was **thunderous** and went on for **ages**. The party from Fairfield Road **whooped** and **cheered** the loudest and gave their friend Fifi a standing ovation. Even the seagulls **banged** their beaks on the windows to show their appreciation.

There was a **tense** wait while the judges deliberated, but finally the results were announced. In third place was a street dance group called The Twickenham Twisters. The runner-up was a belly-dancing pensioner called Rene the Remarkable. And the winner was, of course . . . Miss Fifi Lampadaire!

The audience erupted, cameras flashed, flowers were presented to a tearful Fifi and she sang her winning song once more to a delirious, entranced Teddington Town Hall.

After such a triumph, things happened very quickly for Fifi. The phone rang constantly with offers of more singing work, and before too long she got herself an agent to guide her career and negotiate her payments.

Fifi's agent (a cigar-smoking woman called Mandy Weird) announced that Fifi would go down very well on cruise ships as the on-board entertainment.

'Alors!' cried Fifi. 'This is my dream, but I have not got the passport to travel! How can I conquer the world with my talent without a passport?' (Passports are what humans need when they go abroad. You have to fill in a long form and send it away to a big office, together with your birth certificate: not really a possibility when you're a poodle.)

'Would a pet passport work?' suggested Mr Bold unwisely.

'A PET passport?' asked an incredulous Fifi. 'Do I look like a PET to you?'

'Well, no,' stammered Mr Bold. 'It's just that you are, you know, well, we all are, at the end of the day, animals. Aren't we?'

'Mon Dieu!' howled Fifi. 'How can you say such things? It is an insult! Fermez la bouche

– maintenant!' And with that she flounced up to her bedroom.

'What did she just say?' asked Mr Bold.

'I think she just told you to "shut your mouth",' said Minnie, who'd been to France on holiday the year before and had learned that particular phrase herself.

Mr Bold shrugged. 'Well, I'm an animal and proud of it. So there,' he said to no one in particular.

What's the difference between a guitar and a fish?

You can't tuna fish!

For the next few days the atmosphere in the Bolds' household was not, for once, a very happy one. Fifi's mood did not improve and tearful outbursts and door slamming happened almost hourly. She wanted to work on a cruise ship. She MUST have a passport . . .

In the end Mr McNumpty could stand it no more. 'Right,' he sighed. 'There's only one thing for it.' He had a strange look of grim determination on his face.

'What are you going to do?' asked Uncle Tony.

'I am going to get that poor Fifi a passport.'

'How can you?'

Mr McNumpty tapped the side of his nose. 'Ask no questions and I'll tell you no lies,' he said to his pal.

'You're not going to do anything dangerous, are you?' Nigel McNumpty was Tony's best friend, and Tony didn't like the idea of him getting into trouble.

'Don't worry. I won't be gone long.'

Now Mr McNumpty had been around a long time and liked to consider himself older and wiser than most. When he was younger he used to go drinking in a pub on the Old Kent Road where you could, at a price, acquire almost anything. In the back bar, called 'the snug', you would always find two notorious brothers called 'The Claws'. Their ruthlessness was as legendary as their criminal activities. Although they were small, if anyone annoyed them or crossed them in any way, revenge would be swift and vicious. A man once accidentally knocked over one of the brothers' drink and they both leaped off their chairs and bit the poor chap on the ankles. Even drew blood! You didn't mess with the Claw Brothers. Everyone knew that.

But Nigel McNumpty had always got on well with the two brothers. They shared a secret, you see. Yes, that's right: the Claws were animals in disguise too. Weasels. Now there was nothing else for it, Mr McNumpty would have to go and pay his old friends a visit.

Mr McNumpty really didn't like taking risks or being dishonest in any way, but he could see no other way round the passport situation – to get a passport Fifi was going to need a fake birth certificate. Without it, her budding career was as good as over. He had to help. From his bedside drawer he took several hundred pounds from his secret savings, picked up one of Fifi's new publicity photos, took a deep breath and slipped out of the house.

A few days later he presented an incredulous Fifi with her passport and she wept and whooped with joy. But however many questions everyone asked, Mr McNumpty refused to say exactly how he had got it for her.

'Sometimes it is best not to know,' he said sagely. 'All that matters is that you can now travel and sing for people anywhere in the world. I couldn't let a little thing like you not being human get in the way of that.'

At last, happiness was restored at the Bolds', all thanks to Mr McNumpty.

Chapter

I told you a lot happens in this book, didn't I? It's action-packed, if I say so myself! But as you can probably tell, things are slowly drawing to a conclusion.

Mr and Mrs Bold, the twins, Mr McNumpty, Miranda and Tony carried on with their laughter-filled lives at Numbers 39 and 41 Fairfield Road, Teddington, until eventually most of the visitors who moved into the Bolds' house at the beginning of this book were ready to move on. Here's what happened to them:

Roger the sheep passed his childcare exams and went to work as a nanny with a family in the Cotswolds, where he looked after three very nice, well-spoken children while their parents were at work.

Minty and Molly the racehorses, together with Hamish, had great success with their gardening business (no one guessed the secret of what made the flowers thrive so well) and eventually they became chief gardeners for Regent's Park in London. The job came with a sweet little house, so they moved in there and were very happy indeed.

Fifi the French poodle started her work singing on the cruise ships, where she was, of course, a huge hit. She loved singing, but she also loved travelling and seeing all the different countries.

Bonjour

Mes amis, having a wonderful time. Wish you were here.

Fifi ♡ xxxxxxxxxxxx x

To The Boldes
41 Fairfield Rd
Teddington
UK

The cat and her kittens had no intention of pretending to be humans. They just wanted a place to stay – so they weren't going anywhere. And the turtle? Well, he moved from the washing machine to a pond Mr McNumpty dug in the garden – but he wasn't going any further than that.

That just left Sheila the crocodile . . .

Sheila wasn't doing quite so well. She had yet to find her place in the world and showed no sign of moving on. The Bolds all treated her as kindly as ever, but the truth was that she just wasn't enjoying life in Teddington and longed to swim free and wild somewhere. Living life as a human didn't suit her. Her escape from the sewers seemed to have been a mistake. She was miserable and inconsolable.

When Fifi came home to Teddington between engagements, she did her very best to cheer Sheila up but her friend remained sad and distant.

Then one day, just before she was due to leave for her next cruise-ship booking in Cairo on the River Nile, Fifi had an idea. She looked Sheila up and down and asked: 'Sheila, ma chèrie, can you hold your tail in your mouth?'

'Er, yes, of course,' replied Sheila in surprise at the unusual question. She curled her tail towards her head and grabbed it between her teeth. 'Like this?' she managed to say.

'Oui! Très interesting,' murmured Fifi. 'I think I may have had an idea. Perhaps une idée merveilleuse!'

The next day the whole Bold household went to the airport to see Fifi off on her trip to Egypt. They helped her carry her luggage to the check-in, and waved her goodbye as she disappeared through departures, a smart crocodile bag slung over her shoulder as hand luggage.

Mrs Bold wiped a tear from her eye. 'I do hope Fifi's plan works,' she said.

Can you guess the end of this story? As I can't hear your answer to the question I'd better tell you, just in case.

A week later a letter arrived at 41 Fairfield Road addressed to Les Bolds. A letter with an Egyptian stamp on it . . .

'A letter from Fifi!' cried Mrs Bold excitedly. 'Gather round, everyone, and I'll read it out loud!' Mr Bold, the twins, their friend Minnie, Mr McNumpty, Uncle Tony and Miranda all crowded into the kitchen to hear the news.

Her hands shaking with nerves, Mrs Bold opened the letter, cleared her throat and read what Fifi had written:

Mes chers amis,

Bonjour from sunny Egypt!

I have so much to tell you. Most importantly I am singing better than ever and everyone loves me. I had three encores last night. Three! My talent is recognised here and I'm the talk of Egypt.

But on to other matters. Sheila's disguise as a shoulder bag worked brilliantly and nobody suspected a thing as I got on the plane. On board I placed her carefully in the overhead locker where she was able to release her tail from her mouth and relax during the flight.

There was just one sticky moment when someone placed their bag of ham sandwiches and crisps in the locker during take-off and Sheila scoffed them. When the passenger went to look for them later he was quite mystified and looked accusingly around at everyone, but luckily he didn't suspect the truth.

When we got to Cairo I got Sheila out and slung her over my shoulder as before. I was quite nervous going through Customs but all went well. A woman at the baggage carousel said, 'What a lovely bag. Is it real?' I couldn't help but chuckle to myself, I can tell you!

After a long bus trip we finally boarded the cruise ship on the River Nile. Safely in my cabin Sheila, poor thing, almost collapsed with thirst and exhaustion, and her skin was terribly dry, so I put her in the shower where she stayed rehydrating for a good couple of hours. She was also starving hungry, so I went to the all-you-can-eat buffet and piled my tray high with tasty, meaty morsels that I brought back to the cabin. She devoured the lot in about a minute!

We waited a couple of days, until the cruise ship was well away from the city and the waters of the Nile looked clean and fresh. We were almost ready for the final part of my plan. I awoke in the middle of the night to find Sheila looking longingly out of the porthole at the river, taking deep breaths of fresh air and humming to herself with joy.

'Fifi, dear, I think this might be the perfect spot, don't you agree? Look how beautiful it is! I'm itching to swim out there,' she said earnestly.

I must admit we were both a little tearful, knowing we would never see each other ever again.

'But this is what I want,' said Sheila firmly. 'To live in the wild, as a crocodile, with other crocodiles. To swim, to snap, to meet a husband, have baby crocodiles and to be FREE!'

'Je sais,' I told her. 'I know. And I wish you, Sheila, a très long and happy life.' I popped her over my shoulder one last time and we made our way onto the deck. No one was about. It was a warm, starry night.

'Good luck, Sheila!' I whispered. 'From me, the Bolds and everyone at Fairfield Road. Bonne chance! Remember us!'

'I will. I always will,' she said. 'Thank you, and please be sure to give everyone my love.' And with that she slipped silently over the side of the ship and into the Nile. I watched as a few bubbles rose to the surface, saw her big tail flick once in the air, as if she was waving goodbye, and then she was gone.

I will write again soon.

Tout mon amour,

Fifi.

X

Mrs Bold folded the letter, slid it back in its envelope and placed it on the mantelpiece.

Everyone was quiet for a moment, until Mr Bold said, 'Well, that worked out well, then. Three cheers for Sheila!'

'Hip hip?'

'Hip hip?'

'Hip hip?'

'Hooray!'

'Hooray!'

'HOORAY!'

But how quiet the house seemed, with everyone gone. Too quiet. No Sheila swishing about in the bathroom, no Fifi preening in front of the mirror in the hallway, no Roger pottering about and playing games with the twins, and no Minty and Molly with their nervous whinnying, clattering up and down the stairs.

Betty and Bobby wandered into the garden and sat on the lawn to think.

'Isn't it lovely that all our friends have started their new lives?' said Betty, looking at the roses which were starting to fade without Molly and Minty's special fertilizer.

'S'pose,' said Bobby forlornly. 'I hope they come and see us soon, though. I really miss them.'

'Well, Mum says everyone – apart from Sheila – has promised to come back to Teddington for Christmas,' Betty reminded him. 'We'll all be together again. Don't be sad.'

'Moo!' came the reply.

'Moo to you too!' said Betty indignantly.

'I didn't say "Moo"!' said Bobby.

'You did too moo!' Betty argued.

'Moo! Mooooo!'

The twins realised the moo-ing noise was coming from behind them. They turned to look and there, poking through the privet hedge, was a big ginger cow's head.

'Hello,' said Betty. 'Can we help you?'

'I do hope so.' The poor cow sounded rather bunged up. 'Is this the Bolds' residence? My name is Kirsty. I have a terrible problem, you see. I'm a cow who has hay fever. I simply cannot stay another moment in a field. And I hear on the grapevine that you now have some vacancies . . . ?'

'Er, yes, we do,' said Betty excitedly. 'I'd have to ask my mum and dad first though.'

'I thought, if I could learn to behave like a human being, then maybe I could get a job in an office. Secretary? Bank clerk? I don't really mind as long as it's air-conditioned and I can escape from that dreadful pollen!'

Just then Mr and Mrs Bold came strolling into the garden, holding hands and laughing as usual.

'Oh, Fred, you are a scream!' howled Mrs Bold.

'Ah, what have we here?' said Mr Bold when he spotted the ginger cow.

'Dad, Mum, come and meet Kirsty. Can she stay with us?' asked Bobby.

'Of course you may, Kirsty!' said Mrs Bold. 'Have you come far?'

'Thank you so much,' said the grateful cow. 'I've come from a farm in Dorset.'

'Welcome to the Bolds',' said Mr Bold. 'Help yourself to the lawn. Mind if I ask you a few questions first?'

'Certainly,' blinked Kirsty.

All the Bolds **laughed** heartily, and Kirsty joined in. But there were more jokes to come. Lots more . . .

By now all the Bolds were rolling on their backs, laughing **helplessly** and holding their sides.

What do cows like to do
at amoosement parks?

Ride the
Roller Cow-ster!

What do you get
if you cross two cows
with a flock of ducks?

Milk and
quackers!

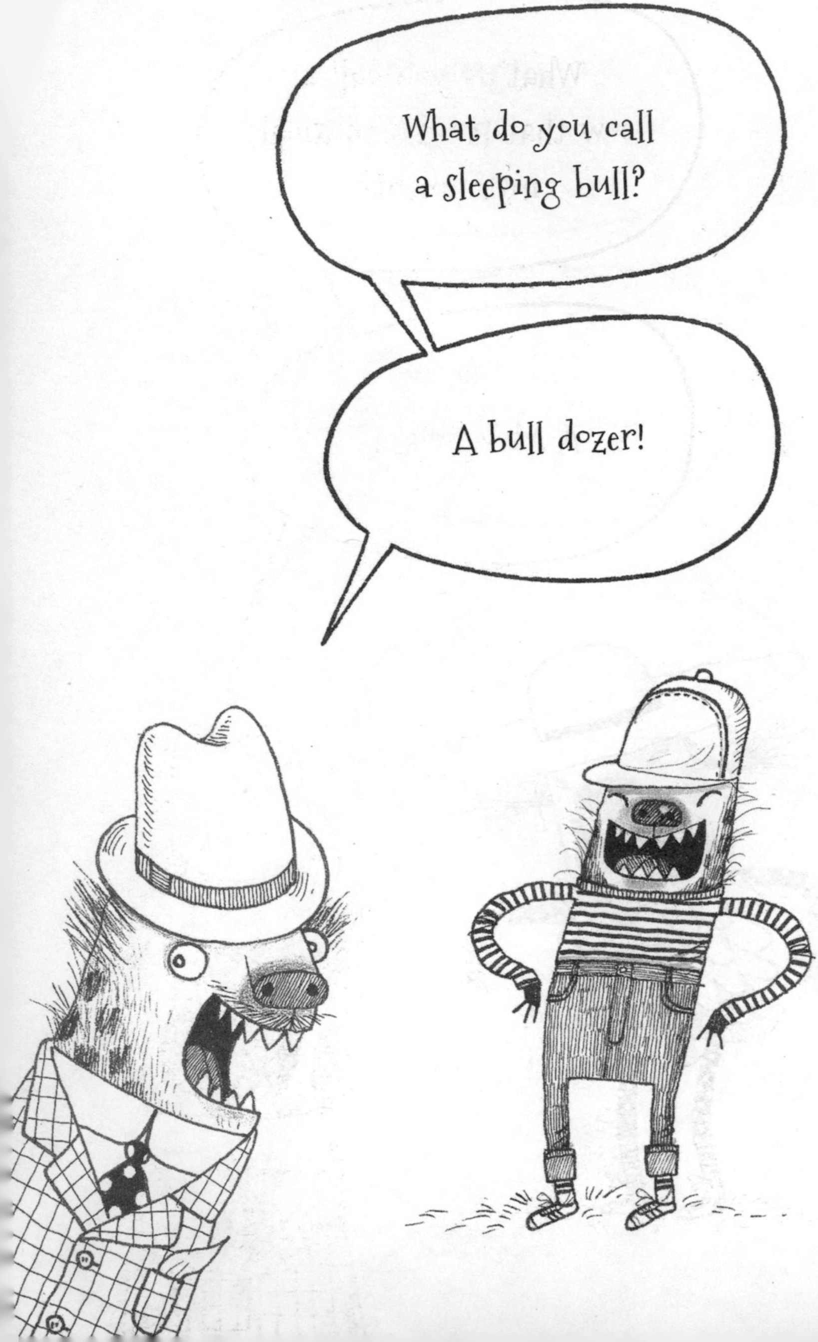
What do you call a sleeping bull?
A bull dozer!

Goodness, thought Kirsty to herself. It was going to be a lot of fun living here.

Kirsty was right, of course. In fact, it's nonstop fun at the Bolds'. We know that, don't we?

Just don't tell the grown-ups. We don't want them spoiling it.

The End

MR BOLD'S JOKES

Why did the banana go to the doctor?
Because he wasn't peeling well!

Why did the jelly wobble?
Because it saw the milk shake!

Where do bees go to the bathroom?
At the BP station!

What do you call a sewer expert?
A conna-sewer!

What do cows like to do at amoosement parks?
Ride the Roller Cow-ster!

What do you get if you cross an angry sheep with a grumpy cow?
An animal that's in a baaaaaad moooood!

Why did the singer climb the ladder?
To reach the high notes!

What do you give a sick horse?
Horse stirrup!

What happened to the man who put his false teeth in backwards?
He ate himself!

How do you make a baby sleep on a space ship?
You rocket!

Did you hear the joke about the broken egg?
Yes, it cracked me up!

Why did the teacher turn the lights on?
Because her pupils were so DIM!

Why do gorillas have such big fingers?
Because they have such big nostrils!

What's worse than a crocodile with toothache?
A centipede with athlete's foot!

Why did the chicken cross the playground?
To get to the other SLIDE!

What did the mayonnaise say when someone opened the refrigerator door?
'Close the door, I am dressing!'

What's the difference between a horse and a duck?
One goes quick, the other goes quack!

What do you call a pony with a sore throat?
A little hoarse!

Did you hear about the man who plugged his electric blanket into the toaster?
He kept popping out of bed all night!

What did the shoes say to the hat?
You go on a-head, I'll follow you on foot!

What do you call a man with a seagull on his head?
Cliff!

Knock knock.
Who's there?
Police.
Police who?
Police hurry up it's cold outside!

What's the difference between a guitar and a fish?
You can't tuna fish!

Why did the cow cross the road?
To get to the udder side!

Why do cows wear bells?
Because their horns don't work!

What sport do horses like to play?
Stable tennis!

What sort of cake does a baker with a cold make?
A cough-ee cake!

What do you get if you cross two cows with a flock of ducks?
Milk and quackers!

What do you call a cow that plays a musical instrument?
A Moo-sician!

Knock knock.
Who's there?
Cargo.
Cargo who?
Car go beep beep!

When Julian Clary isn't having a silly time dressing up and telling jokes on stage, he loves to be at home with his pets. He has lots of them: dogs, cats, ducks and chickens. His life-long love of animals inspired him to tell a story about what would happen if they pretended to be like us. Julian loves going on tour around the country reading his books aloud to children and animals.

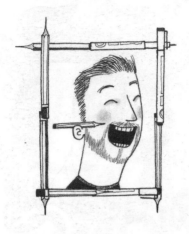

David Roberts always loved to draw and paint as a child, and when he grew up his talents took him all the way to Hong Kong where he got a job making beautiful hats. But he always wanted to illustrate children's books, and so he came back to England to work with the finest authors in the land. David loves drawing animals and clothes and hats, so what could be better than a book about animals *in* clothes and hats?

THE BOLDS

Illustrated by David Roberts

By Julian Clary

The Bolds are just like you and me: they live in a house, they have jobs and they love to have a bit of a giggle. But this family has one great big hairy secret – they're hyenas.

So far, the Bolds have managed to keep things under wraps. But the nosy man next door smells a rat. Will the Bolds be able to keep their secret safe?

'Joyful' *Telegraph*
'Glorious' *Daily Mail*
'Heaps of fun' *Heat*

9781783443055   £6.99